Dear Reader,

The holiday season is fast approaching, and all of us here at the Reader Service would like to take this opportunity to extend our warmest wishes to you and your loved ones.

As a special holiday gift, our editors have selected this wonderful Christmas story, *Miracle on I-40,* to give to you, our Reader Service members. We hope you will enjoy reading this story as much as we have enjoyed giving it to you.

All the best for a very merry Christmas and a happy and prosperous New Year!

Season's Greetings,

Rose Hilliard

D0036810

MIRACLE
On I-40

CURTISS ANN MATLOCK

Silhouette Books

Published by Silhouette Books
America's Publisher of Contemporary Romance

SILHOUETTE BOOKS

ISBN 0-373-15287-6

MIRACLE ON I-40

Copyright © 1988 by Curtiss Ann Matlock
Originally published in Silhouette Christmas Stories
Copyright © 1988 by Silhouette Books

Chapter One

Lacey paused at Web Connor's table and swirled the steaming coffee around in the pot. "More coffee, Web?" she asked. Web had already downed five cups and by all rights should have been swirling himself.

Web shook his head and smiled. "No, gotta get going. Thank you just the same." He began to slide his hefty frame from the red vinyl seat. "Gerald outdid himself on that pie today."

"Glad you enjoyed it, Web. See you soon," Lacey called after him as he wound his way among Formica-topped tables to the door. She began stacking the dirty dishes, and beneath Web's plate she found a twenty-dollar bill.

She stared at the bill a moment, then jerked it up and pivoted. Web was just pushing through the glass doors. "Web!" she called, waving the bill in the air. "Wait! This is a twenty."

He turned and called back gruffly, "I can see that. You think I haven't noticed how you always cut me the biggest piece of pie and make sure my steak's done just right?" He raised a hand. "Merry Christmas from me and Milly." Then he was out the door.

Lacey watched him walking rapidly away toward the tractor-trailer rig he drove for Inman Trucking, the wind tugging at his red-plaid jacket. Turning again to the table, she blinked to clear her vision and slipped the bill into her apron pocket, then finished gathering the dishes.

Lacey Bryant waited tables at Gerald's Truck Stop Restaurant, part of a large complex that served truckers and other drivers from nearby Interstate 40, which cut right through Albuquerque, New Mexico. A mix of modern efficiency and homey friendliness, Gerald's did a thriving business with the locals, too. Lacey was on a first-name basis with many of her customers.

The restaurant was a gay place at Christmastime, with so many people bustling in—families heading home or to visit relatives, truckers trying to make as many hauls as possible before Christmas Day, women taking a break from their shopping. Christmas songs played from the jukebox. Silver garlands swooped over the windows and doorframes. Tiny multicolored lights blinked on the green plastic tree. Shiny stars and bright Mexican piñatas hung from the ceiling. Already Gerald had allowed a few small children the treat of breaking a piñata and gathering up the candy that rained across the floor.

Lacey loved the way customers acted at this season. Everyone seemed to smile for no particular reason— didn't matter whether they knew each other or not. Folks chatted freely, confided their holiday plans. Even Harry Cummings smiled, and he was about as sour as they came.

Lacey just plain loved Christmas. She had ever since she could remember. It was as if magic descended on her world at this time, swelling her heart with invincible joy.

One hand balancing the dishes from Web's table, the other bearing the coffeepot, Lacey headed behind the counter. She dumped the dishes into the waiting plastic pan and glanced at the clock. Four-ten. She would be off at five, making it a ten-hour day. She'd been glad for the extra hours; it was her last day before taking off for two weeks, and she needed all the money she could earn.

Lacey had been putting in lots of overtime for the past three months. There were Christmas presents to buy for her children, and like the singer now crooning from the jukebox, she was going home for Christmas.

Thinking of the trip gave her pause, and she stood for a moment with a wet dishrag held in midair as her thoughts traveled across miles and years. There was a distinct possibility that she might not be welcome at the home where she'd grown up, that her father might turn her away. But she refused to dwell on the possibility. It was Christmas, after all. And Lacey considered it her greatest strength, the thing that enabled her not only to survive but to enjoy life, that she never, *never* dwelled on the less than best that could happen.

The swinging door to the kitchen burst open.

"Doin' okay out here?" Jolene asked. She was the only other waitress on duty through the quieter afternoon hours between the lunch and dinner rushes.

"Doing fine," Lacey said. Giving Jolene a wry smile, she added, "Someday you'll have to teach me your trick for keeping all the customers away from your tables and sitting at mine."

"It's a secret I shall never reveal." Jolene pranced away to the jukebox. Thirty seconds later Glen Campbell was singing about Santa coming to town.

"Does that guy always slide his cup back and forth like that?" Jolene asked when she joined Lacey behind the counter. She inclined her head toward the booth where a lanky J. B. Hunt driver sat.

Lacey nodded and slipped the funnel from the coffee machine. "He has ever since he came in."

"Glad he's over there. If he was any closer, I think I'd scream at him." Jolene reached into the cabinet for the coffee filters and plunked the box onto the counter. "Your eyes are lit up like Christmas trees."

Lacey couldn't help smiling broadly as she discarded the used filter. "I've made enough in tips to get Jon the remote-control car he wants for Christmas—the exact one! I've been putting off buying another model, hoping I could get the real thing."

"That's good, honey. How *are* the kids? Are they getting excited about the trip?"

"Anna has a cold. And yes and no to excitement," Lacey answered. She sloshed the plastic funnel around in the soapy water, then rinsed it. "I didn't bother with a tree this year, since we're not going to be home, and the kids were none too happy about that. But on the whole, they see the trip as an adventure. They've told everyone—and I mean everyone, including the UPS delivery man—that they'll be riding across country in a big eighteen-wheel truck, and they keep asking all kinds of questions about their grandparents and what things were like when I was a kid." She dried the funnel.

"Did you ever tell them about the problem between you and your parents?" Jolene asked.

Lacey sighed. "I tried, but every time I lost my nerve. I was afraid of prejudicing the kids against their grandparents or making them disappointed in me. I ended up saying that Grandma and Grandpa didn't know we were coming and it was to be a surprise."

Jolene gave a nod of understanding. "I guess it would be a pretty touchy subject, especially for Jon. You all set for the trip?"

Lacey filled the filter with fresh-ground coffee. "I have a few last-minute things to get tonight—Jon's car, nose drops for Anna and new underwear for me." She jammed the filter into the machine. "Why is it that women's underwear doesn't seem to survive more than a few launderings these days?"

Jolene shrugged and studied her bitten-off fingernails. "Pate still picking you up at six tomorrow morning?"

Lacey glanced at the clock and felt her stomach tighten. "I guess so. I was sort of expecting him to call or drop by today, he hasn't."

"If Pate told you six tomorrow morning, he'll be there at five to," Jolene assured her. "He's as punctual as the sunrise."

"I know." Lacey nodded.

She thought about Pate and all his kindnesses, the latest being his offer to drive her and the children all the way to North Carolina and back on his truck route. Without that ride, she and the kids would not be making the journey. She was a single mother, the sole support of her two growing children. She already had to stretch the budget for clothes, dentist's visits, school field trips and to try to put a little aside for a rainy day. Due to a hefty and unexpected car repair bill, her rainy-day money at the moment was all but nonexistent, and she simply had to count on sunshine.

"You know," Jolene mused, "Pate's a lot like my Frank. You could do worse."

"Oh, Jolene!" Lacey laughed and adjusted the glass pot beneath the stream of steaming coffee. "It's not like that with us. Pate's more like a father to me."

"What do you think Frank is to me? That and a lot more. Older men can give you what younger ones never

can—in more ways than one, if you get my drift." Jolene gave her a knowing look. "It's a thought."

"No, it's not," Lacey said firmly.

"Okay—don't get touchy." Jolene's gaze moved past
Lacey's shoulder, and a slow, welcoming smile slipped
across her face. When her friend lifted her hand to
wave, Lacey turned to see a regular customer they all
knew simply as Cooper pushing through the glass
doors.

"Mmm, he's a sight to warm a woman's heart," Jolene said in a hoarse whisper. "And he'll sit at your table, of course." She winked and pushed away from the
counter.

Knowing Jolene intended to retreat to the kitchen
again, Lacey reached for the coffeepot. "Since I've got
a new customer to take care of, you can refill coffee
cups," she said sweetly.

Jolene gave a throaty chuckle and took the glass pot.
Lacey walked over to grab a menu, even though it was
probably a waste of time. Cooper would either order the
Texas T-bone or the Piping Hot Chili. For the past four
years she'd been serving him, it had been one of the two.
Of course, there *had* been that time he'd ordered
breakfast.

As she turned, she was surprised to see that Cooper
had slipped onto a stool at the counter. It struck her as
strange; Cooper always sat in a booth, usually the front
corner one with a good view of the parking lot. Equally
unusual, he was watching her expectantly.

"Good afternoon." She set the menu in front of him
and looked into his dark eyes, finding an odd expression there. A hesitancy, a nervousness.

Cooper extended the folded piece of paper Pate had
given him and said, "From Pate." The note would ex-

plain, so he didn't think he needed to say more at this point.

Lacey's pale, slim, feminine fingers seemed a stark contrast to his large, rough, dark ones as she slowly took the note. Confusion and apprehension clouded her eyes. Cooper noticed they were the color of spring grass just before she lowered them to the paper.

He ran his gaze over her curly brown hair and ivory cheeks and for the hundredth time asked himself how he'd gotten hooked into doing this. Maybe he would escape his own foolish sentimentality; maybe she would simply refuse to go now.

Either she was a slow reader or she couldn't comprehend the words the first time, because it seemed to take her an inordinately long time to read the few words. Cooper knew what was in the note; he'd read it, unashamedly.

Dear Lacey,
   Cooper will explain about me. He will also take you to North Carolina right along with hauling my payload on up to Washington. Cooper is a good man. I trust him with my life. So I can trust him with yours, too. Have a good Christmas. Hope everything turns out the way you want.

Love,
Pate

Cooper felt a bit of embarrassment over the high praise. And he wondered about it. He didn't think anyone, even a friend like Pate, knew him well enough to form such an opinion.

After what seemed like a very long time, Lacey raised her eyes to him. Her face was white, her green eyes filled with confusion. "What..." She stopped the question and waited.

Just as Cooper opened his mouth to explain about Pate, a tall, good-looking guy appeared at his shoulder, standing in front of the cash register.

"Excuse me," Lacey said.

She stepped behind the register to take the man's payment. The guy called her "honey" and attempted to chat in an overly familiar way. She called him politely by name—Lyle—but seemed to put him in his place by being cold as ice.

Cooper looked at her and couldn't blame the guy for flirting. Lacey was a pretty woman, always friendly, and Cooper chose to sit at one of her tables when he could because she was a damned good waitress.

He recalled several times when he'd considered asking her out. Well, it'd been more than several. Fact was, more than once when he'd looked at her, she'd looked back. There'd been mutual interest. But something told Cooper she could cause him a lot of complications, so he'd never asked her and had kept to himself. He wondered how serious her relationship with Pate was. He knew they were real friendly, spent time together.

"It iced up on us in Santa Fe yesterday evening. Pate slipped and fell down the front stairs of his apartment," Cooper told her when she returned. He watched distress replace the confusion in her eyes. "Broke his leg bad enough to require a hospital stay. I told him I'd haul his payload and take *you* on to this place in North Carolina."

"Pine Grove," Lacey said.

"Yeah. He said west side of Raleigh."

She nodded, a faraway, thoughtful expression on her face. Then she blinked and focused on him. Maybe now she'd say she wouldn't go. Cooper waited.

"Pate's in the hospital?" she asked.

Cooper nodded. "But he should be released day after tomorrow. His son's family is flying out from Richmond to spend Christmas with him and take care of him."

"Oh." Now she was studying him closely. The next instant she turned quickly and reached for the coffeepot. "Want some coffee?" she asked.

Cooper stood and stretched, saying, "That and the chili dinner. I'll sit over there." He inclined his head toward the corner booth. He waited while she poured him the coffee, then he took the cup. For an instant he looked into her green eyes. The way she kept studying him was annoying. Why didn't she just say she'd changed her mind about going East?

Lacey bent to write his order on her pad and listened to his boots scuff the tile as he walked to his usual booth.

What was she going to do now? she asked herself. The children were counting on going. It was way past time they met their grandparents and aunt and uncle and cousins. Her sister was planning on their Christmas Eve arrival, and would be watching, ever so discreetly, out the big front window. And Lacey hungered to see the home where she'd grown up, to see her parents. She longed for the chance to make things right with her father.

"So, what's the big deal?" Jolene asked when Lacey explained the situation to her. They were in the kitchen, where Lacey was putting together a salad for Cooper.

"Cooper isn't Pate," Lacey said. "Pate...well, we're good friends. I wasn't imposing on him—it's not imposing on a good friend. And you didn't see Cooper's face. He doesn't want to do this. He's only doing it for Pate."

"Oh, Cooper always looks grumpy. The man's afraid to be friendly, afraid people will find out he's got as big a soft spot as everyone else."

"Where in the world did you get that idea?"

"I've been out with him."

Lacey stared at her friend. "When?"

"Oh, about three years ago—before I met Frank." Jolene handed Lacey the salad dressing. "Went out with him twice, as a matter of fact. Once to a show, then to a show and dinner. He's a real gentleman—good manners and all—but he's a loner. Not the marrying kind, if you know what I mean. Still, he's a good guy."

"What's his first name?" Lacey asked.

Jolene frowned. "I don't know."

"You went out with him twice and never learned his first name? Didn't you ask?"

Jolene shook her head. "He's just Cooper. Everyone calls him Cooper. Maybe that *is* his first name. And why would I need to know? Two shows and dinner doesn't mean marriage." Jolene pointed a finger at Lacey. "You want to go home—you need to go home. Now's your chance, and my advice is to take it, because you're not going to get another like it. Besides, what will you tell the kids? Sorry, it's all off? Then they'd have to tell their friends, *and* the UPS man, that their bragging was all lies."

"Thanks, Jolene," Lacey said dryly, and thrust the bowl of salad toward her. "You take this to him. I need a few minutes to think this thing through."

Much of what Jolene had said was true, Lacey reflected. She imagined Jon's and Anna's disappointed faces when she told them the trip was off. Lacey herself hated the thought of not going. Beth was expecting her; they would talk and laugh about scrapes they'd gotten into as children. And she missed her mother, who wouldn't be around forever, she reminded herself sadly. And her father—well, it was time one of them made an effort at reconciliation.

Riding back East with Pate had been a perfect arrangement. Pate Andrews was around fifty, widowed and lived alone up in Santa Fe. His job as a trucker brought him into Gerald's on a regular basis, and over the years he and Lacey had formed a special kind of friendship. As Lacey once told Jolene, Pate had taken the place of the father she didn't have, the grandfather the children had never met.

When she discovered he was driving back East for the holidays, she hadn't hesitated to ask him the big favor of taking her and the children along. She'd even explained her intentions. Pate hadn't laughed or told her she was being foolish. He'd told her he'd fix it with his company.

But hitching a ride with Cooper wasn't the same. She had no doubt as to his character; Pate wouldn't have set it up if Cooper wasn't completely trustworthy. It was just that Lacey hardly knew Cooper. He wasn't a friend. How could she impose so much on a man who was almost a complete stranger?

A loud clanging made her jump. The cook had dropped a pan. Needing something to do with her hands, Lacey walked over to stir the chili and the potato and vegetable soups.

She tried to recall what she knew of Cooper. Pate and he were friends; they often ate together at the restaurant. Cooper seemed to be respected by the other drivers; while not overly friendly, apparently he was well-known and liked.

Lacey knew little else, and what little she did know was mostly impressions. She'd been waiting on Cooper since she'd started working at Gerald's four years earlier, yet she didn't even know whether Cooper was his first name, his last or a nickname. He was polite but seemed to wear a big invisible sign that said No Trespassing.

Though, Lacey admitted reluctantly, she'd felt his low-keyed interest on more than one occasion, and she'd be lying if she didn't say she found him attractive. But she'd never considered Cooper a man to get involved with.

The qualities that made him extremely attractive to women, including herself—a rugged handsomeness, an aura of strength, even a hint of danger—made Lacey equally leery of him. She'd want a gentle, caring man— if ever she got around to having time for a relationship. It wasn't easy, what with raising and supporting two children.

Jolene burst through the door, bearing the big plastic dishpan. She set it on a counter and whirled to hold out several bills toward Lacey.

"Here's your tip from that man who favored sliding his cup around. He was right nice, too," she said. "Now, you'd better get Cooper his chili. It doesn't take long to eat that small salad. And no, I'm not taking it."

Absolutely no closer to a decision, Lacey grabbed the big plate of thick chili and cheese the cook had prepared, took a deep breath and pushed through the swinging door.

As she walked toward Cooper, her heart thudded within her breast. In an instant she noted his thick hair and coarse mustache, both so dark brown they were almost black. That he was a lean hard-muscled man was plainly evident, even though he wore a flannel shirt over a long-sleeved undershirt. He had to have heard her footsteps, but he didn't so much as lift his head from his newspaper. The austere impression again came to the fore, and Lacey liked neither of the choices she faced.

She stopped at his table and waited for him to look up at her. Slowly he raised his gaze to meet hers. His dark brown eyes reflected curiosity.

His gaze dropped to the plate she held. Quickly he folded his paper and put it aside. Lacey set the plate before him, hesitated, then slipped into the opposite seat.

"How did Pate seem when you left him?" she asked as she folded her hands and forced them to rest quietly atop the table.

Cooper shook dried hot pepper atop his chili and cheese. "He was wide awake and flirting with the nurse." He didn't look up at her.

Lacey stared at him. It was either go with him—or not go at all. The latter would mean she didn't know when she would get to see her family or when the children would meet their grandma and grandpa.

"You going or not?"

Cooper's voice startled her, and Lacey blinked, realizing she'd been staring at him without really seeing him. Now his dark eyes seemed to bore into her, demanding an answer.

She licked her lips. "I hate to bother you...."

"Look—" he held his knife like a pointer "—I told Pate I'd take you. The deal is still on, just like before, and I'll probably get you there a bit faster than Pate would have. It's not like it was with Pate—I ain't Pate—but it is a ride. Now, do you want to go?"

Lacey stared into those dark, forbidding eyes and felt the squeeze of being caught between the proverbial rock and a hard place.

"I'd be very grateful for the ride," she said.

Something flickered in his eyes. Surprise? Dismay? Lacey wasn't certain, and immediately the cold, blank expression reclaimed his features.

"Okay" was all he said before returning his attention to his chili.

Lacey shifted in her seat. She was reluctant to pressure him about particulars, such as the time and place of pickup. It seemed rude of him not to volunteer the information. She stared at him, but he didn't lift his gaze.

"Pate was going to pick me up at home at six o'clock tomorrow morning," she said at last. She felt ridiculously like a beggar and hated it. Why in the world was the man so purposely disagreeable? Was common cordiality against his principles?

"I'll meet you here at the restaurant at five," Cooper said without looking up. "I like to get an early start."

Lacey opened her mouth in surprise, then closed it and quickly masked her dismay. "Fine," she said with a brief nod. She rose and walked stiffly away.

Perhaps she should simply not go, she thought, her mind whirling. But the results of such a decision were even less appealing than driving sixteen hundred miles with a rude lump of a man.

She sighed. She had chosen the lesser of two evils, she supposed. And now she'd have to spend three whole days in the confines of a tractor-trailer rig with two active children and Mr. Delightful. She might spend most of that time keeping the children and herself out of his way. What fun!

Chapter Two

Lacey's shift ended before Cooper finished his dinner. She stopped by his table, braving the tight-lipped dragon, to ask the name of the hospital Pate was in.

When she said, "See you in the morning," he gave a short nod and a grunt.

He wasn't all that handsome a man, Lacey decided. Looks weren't everything.

She drove through the heavy traffic, mentally reviewing the details that needed to be taken care of before morning. She'd pretty much cleared out the refrigerator; what was left could be tossed out. The newspaper had been stopped . . . mustn't forget to turn down the furnace.

The shopping mall was packed, the store's shelves emptying rapidly. There was only one Tough-Stuff radio-controlled car left at the hobby shop. Lacey spotted it and at that same instant saw another woman heading directly toward it.

With a burst of speed, Lacey sprinted and reached the car first, snatched up the box and held it close. The woman glared at her, and Lacey's cheeks burned from shame. Still, she bit her lip and held the car tightly.

Her embarrassment eased into pleasure as she handed her hard-earned money to the cashier. Jon hadn't asked for another thing, and getting the Tough-Stuff remote-control car would surprise and delight him; he had so few lavish toys. Lacey couldn't help the fact that Anna would not get her longed-for puppy for Christmas, but doing this for Jon helped some. And when they got back home after Christmas, she promised herself, she would see about getting Anna a puppy—even though the thought of such a troublesome critter made her wince.

She laid her packages on the car seat with an audible "Phew!" Her feet and back ached, her hands were stiff and dry, and before her lay dinner still to be prepared, two children to wash and packing to do.

As she drove home, Lacey worried about having overspent. But Anna had really needed socks, and that fancy hair clip hadn't cost *that* much. And Jon's present shoes were disreputable. But she really hadn't needed to buy that belt buckle for Cooper. It'd been a silly, extravagant thing to do. Fifteen dollars. For fifteen dollars she could buy dinner on the trip for her and the kids. Just once, she thought, for an entire month, she'd like to have enough money not to have to scrimp and calculate all the time.

It was spilled milk now, she told herself as she pulled the car into the drive of her duplex apartment. As she opened the front door, both of her children burst from the adjoining apartment, where they stayed with Susan Price during the school holiday break. Lacey called a greeting to Susan, who stood in the doorway. Jon and Anna surrounded her, pretending to try to peek into the bags as they entered the apartment.

"You'll spoil your Christmas," Lacey cautioned.

"Not me. I won't see my puppy until Christmas morning after Santa brings it," Anna said flatly.

Jon switched on the table lamp and held the door for Lacey. "I've told her and told her that Santa won't bring her a puppy this year because of the trip," he said.

"He might." Anna jutted her chin, sniffed and shook her short straight hair.

"Pate won't want a noisy, messy puppy riding all the way back here from North Carolina in his truck," Jon argued.

"He won't care."

"That's enough," Lacey said as she headed down the small hallway to her bedroom. "You two get washed up so you can help with dinner. We've all got a lot to do tonight." She laid the bags on her bed and paused, worrying about how the change in plans might affect the children. It would be best to tell them about Cooper right away and give them as much time as possible to get used to the idea, she decided.

She managed to convey the information, soothe their disappointment about not riding with their friend Pate and get them into bed by eight-thirty.

"What will we do with the puppy Santa brings, Mama?" Anna asked as Lacey tucked the covers around her. "Will Cooper let us bring him home in his truck?"

"Blow," Lacey instructed, holding a tissue to Anna's tiny nose while searching her mind for a response to the question. She stroked the fine hair from her daughter's forehead. "Anna, I told you that your puppy would have to come later, even if we were riding with Pate. A puppy is a delicate thing for Santa Claus to haul around, especially from the cold North Pole. Why, I can't think of anyone who ever got a puppy for Christmas."

"Tammy Henderson did." Anna's big brown eyes dominated her face.

"Well, we'll see." It was one of those situations where a mother couldn't win, Lacey thought. She hated disappointing her daughter, but there seemed no way around it.

In the kitchen she poured a cup of coffee, then called Information for the number of the Santa Fe hospital where Pate was recuperating. She was relieved when his voice, sounding perfectly normal, boomed across the line.

He was obviously surprised and touched to hear from her and kept repeating that he was fine. His son and son's family were due in the following morning, and they were going to have a grand old time.

"And I want you to have a good time, too, Lacey. I'm really sorry to disappoint you, but Cooper will see you and the children safely to Pine Grove. I've known Cooper for nigh on to twenty years now. He's a good, reliable driver. A good man. You can depend on him. I wouldn't have recommended him if I didn't know that."

"I know, Pate," Lacey said. "Thanks for taking care of us."

"Well, I know Cooper can seem a mite disagreeable," Pate drawled. "I know, too, that you'd rather not go with him, but I'm awful glad you are. You need to see your folks, and, Lacey...well, Cooper needs your company on this trip. Holidays are a mighty lonesome time for him."

Lacey silently thought that Cooper didn't seem like the type of man to want, much less need, anyone, but she kept the thought to herself. It would only distress Pate, and that wouldn't change the situation. She hurried to assure him that she and the children would be fine and to wish him a Merry Christmas.

As she replaced the receiver, she realized with chagrin that she'd forgotten to ask Pate what Cooper's full name was.

With a large sigh she reached for the gift she'd bought
Pate, a leather tobacco pouch with his initials em-
bossed on it. She would have to save it for after Christmas.

Shaking away the melancholy that suddenly en-
gulfed her, Lacey briskly began wrapping the few remaining packages. She'd sent some gifts on ahead to her
sister's house, but these precious things she wouldn't
have entrusted to the mails.

There was Jon's car and the battery charger that went
with it and the soft baby doll for Anna. On the doll's
wrist Lacey fastened a real Mickey Mouse watch.
Would the doll and the watch make Anna forget about
a puppy? Lacey frowned as she smoothed down the
doll's hair. No, probably not even a trip to Disney
World would do that.

As she wrapped, Lacey's thoughts turned to her own
childhood. Though their father had been strict, he'd
always seemed to mellow at Christmastime. He'd take
Lacey and Beth out to a friend's land and be unchar-
acteristically patient while they tramped for acres,
searching for just the right tree. Then he'd chop it down
and haul it back to the house.

The shiny green leaves and red berries of holly
gleamed from the mantel and tabletops, and the pun-
gent smell of pine filled the rooms. She missed those
things here in the drier, more rugged climate of Albuquerque. She missed sharing the holidays with her
family. For the past four years every Christmas Eve had
been spent as this evening was: alone.

It was Lacey who picked out the gifts, who wrapped
them, who drank warm apple cider and listened to
Christmas carols and hummed along, no other voice
echoing with hers. And, though she treasured the pres-

ents she received—two nonsensical things made by childish hands, and a lovely gift from Beth every year— she sometimes longed for a special present from a person who knew her well. A treat bought for herself simply wasn't the same.

She unrolled red elf-print paper and placed on it the gift she'd put together for her parents—a photo album chronicling the young lives of Jon and Anna.

The first pictures were of Jon when he'd been only weeks old. A tightness gripped her heart as she paused to look at them. She'd been oh, so foolish, and she fervently hoped she could put things right now.

Lacey had been nineteen and had been going with Shawn Bryant for six months when she got pregnant with Jon. The old saying had been that you couldn't get pregnant on the first experience with sex, but Lacey had.

Her parents had been furious. She could still see her father's face, red with anger and scorn. She'd needed his love and support and had been so bitterly disappointed.

According to her father she'd committed an unpardonable sin and had brought terrible shame upon the family. Her parents had insisted she give the baby up for adoption—something Lacey couldn't bring herself to do. Trying to force her, her father had demanded she follow his edict or get out and fend for herself. She'd left that very afternoon, screaming from the yard that she would never return.

However, pride didn't pay the bills. So she and Shawn had started out like a million other young couples in the world—broke, and with a family on the way. To Shawn's credit, he'd married her without a grumble. He'd enlisted in the air force, a good, steady job, and in the early years they'd moved a number of times. Anna had come along, and they'd become a family of four.

But domestic life brought a sense of confinement rather than contentment to Shawn. There were too many experiences calling him, experiences in which a wife and children had no part. He simply got tired of bills and responsibilities and sleeping with one woman, so four years ago he'd left.

Lacey looked at the picture of Anna's last birthday, her sixth, and smiled sadly. She felt more pity for Shawn than anything else. He'd missed out on so much by not being able to give of himself. And not only didn't he give of himself, but he provided no financial support, either. Though her friends had suggested going through legal channels to get money from him, Lacey had learned that the legalities would end up costing her more money than Shawn would be able to give.

Lacey closed the album and began wrapping it. She thought of Beth, who was expecting her.

Over the years she'd stayed in contact with her sister. During most of those years Beth had urged Lacey to return and attempt a reconciliation with their parents. Lacey had often considered it, but she'd never had the money for the trip. Beth didn't have it, either, and Lacey refused to approach her mother and father for a loan. When she did return, it had to be under her own steam. And of course, there was still that stubborn pride. Why couldn't her parents *ask* her to come home?

Then, two months ago, a letter had come from her mother, at long last. In the letter, her mother had asked Lacey to consider coming home; she'd expressed love for the first time in almost eleven years and a great desire to see her grandchildren. Lacey knew the time had come for going home and rebuilding burned bridges.

But the letter had been from Emily Sawyer alone. Leon Sawyer, Beth admitted, had seemed to grow harder over time. He hadn't spoken Lacey's name since she'd defied his wishes and left, and he grew angry when any other member of the family mentioned her.

Lacey had decided, and Beth had reluctantly agreed, that the best approach to her father was surprise—which meant not telling even her mother that she was coming. She intended to show up on the doorstep with their grandchildren in the flesh. Whether or not it angered her father, she knew he would never do anything to hurt the youngsters, and she hoped with all her heart that her act would tumble the giant wall of bitterness the past had wrought between her and her father. The photo album was a means toward this end as well.

The last gift to be wrapped was the one she'd bought for Cooper in a weak moment that evening. She looked at the shiny metal buckle nested in its small box. It was cast with images of trucking: a smoking tractor-trailer rig, exaggerated tires and highway signs.

For a moment Lacey considered setting it aside. Giving such a personal gift to a man whose full name she didn't even know seemed awfully silly. No doubt she would feel odd when she gave it, and he would feel odd taking it.

But she again cut the elf-print paper to wrap it. The buckle was a token of appreciation. She needed to express that. And it was Christmas, a time for giving, no matter the motive or the relationship.

The final bag to be packed was her own. Lacey found herself pulling everything out of her drawers and closet, despairing over the lack of suitable outfits. All her clothes seemed so worn and out-of-date. And suddenly, looking her best was very important.

She did have one pair of fairly new blue jeans—designer ones bought on sale—and there was the mauve sweater that brought out her skin tones. They would do for the first day. And it wasn't too much trouble to roll her hair. A fleeting anticipation touched her spirit. Would Cooper possibly think her pretty?

She didn't sleep much, tossing and turning, the rollers poking into her scalp no matter what position she tried. And they were the supposedly painless foam ones.

But the next morning her hair looked great—soft, bouncy and shiny. She decided she looked pretty good in her jeans, too, and her efforts served to make her feel confident about the trip ahead as she got herself ready before waking the children.

Maybe yesterday had been simply a bad one for Cooper, making him abnormally grumpy. Maybe today he would welcome them, even be glad to have their company.

"It's a thought," she murmured to the skeptical-looking image in the mirror.

Lacey parked out of the way at Gerald's lot and tucked the key beneath the mat for Jolene, who would return the car to Lacey's duplex later that day.

"Middle of the damn...darn night," Jon grumbled.

Lacey silently agreed as she settled the children in a front booth where she could watch for Cooper's arrival through the big front window. With the night's blackness broken only by the building's silvery outside lights, the window reflected her family's faces.

As often happened, her reflected image startled her. Was that really her with the nice curly hair? Was that woman's figure—shapely and feminine—really hers?

She didn't feel like that inside. Inside she felt quivery and sort of small and uncertain, though she was careful to hide those emotions from her children.

And she wouldn't spend one more second wondering if she were right or wrong in making this trip, she told herself as she tugged a tissue from her tote bag for Anna. She'd gone too far to back out now. And it *was* Christmas season, not a time for fretting.

"Order anything you want, kids," she said, checking her watch. "We have over half an hour."

"It's too early to eat," Jon said.

"Try."

"Three days until Christmas," Anna piped up out of the blue, and gave a bright smile.

Lacey had to smile in return. Things were going to be fine, she told herself. The trip would go well, be an adventure, and at the end her father would open his arms wide for them. She hoped. What would she tell her children if he didn't?

For the next twenty-five minutes Lacey's heartbeat gradually picked up tempo, and her insides began to quiver like a bowl of gelatin, so that when Jon, who'd been craning his neck to peer out the window for the past ten minutes, said, "Did you say Cooper's truck was red?" she almost jumped out of her seat.

"Maroon," she answered, purposely glancing outside with a casualness she didn't feel.

A big, shiny, top-of-the-line Kenworth truck pulling a silver trailer rolled to a stop several yards away. It gleamed in the fluorescent lighting.

Lacey's heart hammered, and a distinctly sinking feeling claimed her when her gaze fell to the Christmas lights draped across the Kenworth's grill. In merry greens, reds and yellows, the lights crudely spelled out

Bah, Humbug. She had to stare at them for approximately thirty seconds to be certain, but that was what they said.

She grasped at the idea that maybe it wasn't Cooper. Plenty of drivers drove such trucks; maybe it was someone else.

Then a figure dressed in a thick vest, shoulders hunched against the cold, with a black Stetson on his head, strode around the front of the truck toward the restaurant. It was Cooper.

When Lacey turned to look at her children, Jon's eyebrows were raised in silent question.

"It's Cooper," she said, stifling a sigh.

"What do those lights say, Mama?" Anna asked.

When Lacey hesitated, Jon filled in. "Bah, Humbug—like old Scrooge." Then he muttered, "I get this funny feeling. . . ." He stopped at Lacey's sharp look.

"Here, Anna, let's get your coat on," she said, casting both children a bright smile. "It's time to go."

Without looking, she mentally pictured Cooper striding into the restaurant. She knew exactly when he entered; she felt a cold breeze—and his gaze. She looked up and across the room.

Cooper was frowning—in fact, his expression was thunderous—as he approached. In the process of zipping Anna's coat, Lacey's fingers stilled. She could do no more than stare at him and wonder what she'd done, because it was obvious he was furious with her.

Cooper knew he'd been hornswoggled. A small voice in the back of his mind told him that it hadn't been by Lacey. It'd been Pate. Pate had neglected to tell him about the kids, and the old guy had done it on purpose. He'd known Cooper wouldn't have gone along with the idea—not at all.

But at the moment Pate wasn't there. And Lacey was. And she should have said something yesterday about there being kids!

"Good morning."

Cooper heard her gentle greeting and fleetingly took in her curling, shiny hair and the softness of her being before turning his gaze to the two pint-sized kids beside her. He didn't say good morning, hello or anything. He didn't know what to say and was afraid of letting the anger within him explode. He returned his gaze to Lacey.

"I'd like you to meet my two children, Cooper," she said, her voice polite and soft, just as if nothing was wrong. "This is Jon—" she touched the boy's shoulder "—and this is Anna."

"Pate didn't say anything about kids." Cooper spoke low, an inner caution clamping down on his vocal chords. But he wanted out of this, and he intended to get out. He wasn't spending three days in the cab of his truck with two wet-nosed kids.

Lacey's eyes widened. She glanced nervously past Cooper, reminding him they were in a public place, then met his gaze again.

"Pate didn't..." Her green eyes searched his. "Pate didn't tell you I had two children—that he was taking all of us to Pine Grove?" Her voice came out hoarse, as if forced from her throat.

"No, ma'am, he didn't." Cooper ground the words out, though he wanted to shout. "And neither did you." So now she would apologize, he thought, and know the trip was off.

"Well, I'm sorry...."

Her eyes were extremely dark against the paleness of her face. She looked confused and apologetic, and a shaft of disappointment touched Cooper. Why did she have to go and have kids? He'd sort of been thinking it might be nice to drive east with her, that having her along might make the stretch ahead seem shorter. A stupid thought that had been.

"I had no idea," she said, seeming to grow taller and straighter right before his eyes. Her voice was soft yet perfectly distinct. "I simply assumed you knew. Pate's note said it was all arranged, and last night when I spoke to him, he didn't say anything."

"No, I guess he didn't," Cooper allowed, his gaze dropping again to the children in front of him.

One was a little girl, about five, a replica of Carla from the vintage Little Rascals shows, with her short, straight brown hair and wide brown eyes. She clung to her mother's leg and regarded him as she would a horned devil. The boy standing next to her was about ten or eleven, with tousled light brown hair and eyes and a body stance that indicated he knew all there was to know in this world.

"Well," Lacey said, "as I said before, these are my children, Jon and Anna." She rested her hand atop the little girl's head and smiled at Cooper. "Kids, this is Mr.—this is Cooper, who's generously agreed to take Pate's place and drive us to Pine Grove."

It wasn't what Cooper had expected. He stared at her, feeling the tables had turned, because now he was the uncertain one. How had she done it? Only seconds ago she'd looked hesitant, vague and definitely on the verge of running. Now she was acting as if everything was going perfectly smoothly, like a blacktopped highway snaking off into the prairie.

What could he say? Cooper thought as he stared into her clear eyes. He'd told Pate he would do this favor for

him; the older man was relying on him. Even though he
had been devious, Cooper still owed him. And he was
a man to pay his debts.

"Come on. We got three days to get there, and I'd
sooner make it in two."

He pivoted and strode toward the restaurant doors,
the sound of "Jingle Bells" following him. Some jerk
had punched the tune into the jukebox, regardless of it
being five o'clock in the morning. *Bah, humbug!* Cooper thought fiercely. Three days in the cab of his rig
with a woman and two wet-nosed kids.

A *beautiful* woman and two wet-nosed kids, he
thought as he paused at the truck's passenger door and
turned to watch Lacey and her children approach. The
thought rubbed salt into the wound. Though Lacey
carried a bulging bag in each hand and another hung
from her shoulder, she walked straight and with firm
steps. The cold breeze blew her hair back from her face;
small gold hoop earrings caught the fluorescent lights.

"Five bags aren't going to fit," he told her when she
came abreast of him. He knew his words were prodded
by a strange desire to rock her self-confidence. If he felt
off-balance, he wanted her to, as well.

"This is a tote bag," she said, indicating the large one
hanging from her shoulder. "And Pate said we could
bring four suitcases."

Cooper was rewarded by the slight quaver in her voice
and the uncertainty that glimmered momentarily in her
eyes. "I ain't Pate," he reminded her.

"You want me to leave one behind?" she said, anger
slipping into her eyes. "Where should I leave it?"

"Here is fine with me."

"I need all four bags—and everything in this tote.
There *are* three of us."

"Rearrange things. There isn't room."

A movement drew his gaze, and Cooper glanced down to see the little girl gaping at him. She looked on the verge of tears, and a twinge of remorse pricked him.

"Okay, fine!" Lacey plunked the two bulging bags onto the black pavement. Kneeling, she unzipped one of them and began jerking clothes from it. A blue sweatshirt flew to the pavement. "I can do without this ... or this...."

A flutter of white followed the sweatshirt, then several frilly pink things that resembled a nightgown and underwear, giving Cooper an uncomfortable feeling in the pit of his stomach. Suddenly he was aware of the cold and of several curious faces peering through the restaurant windows. He knelt and quickly grabbed the scattered clothes, catching a pair of panties that came sailing his way.

"All right!" he said, doing a peculiar bellow through clenched teeth. He thrust the clothes at her. "Put these back in there, and let's get going. At this rate it's going to be six before we get out of here."

Adjusting his hat low on his brow, he strode around the front of the truck, leaving Lacey and her kids to get inside as best they could.

Chapter Three

Lacey watched Cooper disappear around the front of the big truck and contemplated words too ugly to speak. She was embarrassed by her actions and didn't know what to do about the entire situation. Cooper had said he would take them for Pate, yet he wasn't Pate, as he'd reminded her, and he didn't *want* to take them, though he wouldn't say so.

"I don't like him, Mama," Anna said, slipping an arm around Lacey's leg.

"You sure you still want to do this, Mom?" Jon asked.

Lacey looked at him. "Yes." Turning from her son's gaze, she grabbed hold of a handle and hoisted herself up into the vibrating truck. She pulled the two children after her.

In all her years of working at the truck stop, watching the rigs come and go, Lacey had never been inside one. She'd heard of the renowned Kenworth truck, but her imagination hadn't done it justice.

Though the big engine ran, it sent only a gentle, even pleasant, rumble into the truck cab itself. It was cozy, warm. The two high-backed seats were upholstered in thick gray velour and resembled living-room recliners, complete with armrests. Tufted gray vinyl lined the door panels and roof and thick gunmetal-gray carpeting covered the floor.

In the center, behind the chairs, was the opening to the sleeping compartment. Jon could stand in the compartment and move about easily. Lacey paused to stare at the padded vinyl lining the walls and ceiling, the bed that was larger than a double, the luxurious blue bedspread.

"There's a TV!" Jon exclaimed, drawing Lacey's gaze to the small portable on a shelf. Color, no less. There were also speakers in the wall, indicating a stereo system somewhere.

Lacey opened what she thought to be a cabinet, finding a refrigerator instead. Straightening, she came face-to-face with a microwave oven. In a narrow closet hung several pairs of jeans and numerous shirts, a pair of gleaming boots sitting beneath them.

"Where's the shower?" she quipped to Cooper.

His answer was a low grunt. He sat in his seat behind the wheel, apparently engrossed in checking the numerous gauges on the dash, acting as if he were alone in the rig, as no doubt he wished to be.

Lacey squeezed three of their bags into a large, only partially filled cabinet beneath the bed. She was standing in the narrow compartment opening, debating about what to do with the fourth bag, when Cooper appeared at her side.

"All set?" he asked.

Lacey caught the sudden scent of his sweet-musky after-shave. He turned to look at her, his face, lit by the golden glow of the interior lights, only inches away. His eyes were deep and dark, his eyelashes long, his mustache slightly bristly. She realized for the first time how wavy his hair was. His arm came around in front of her, causing her to pull back, as he tossed his hat onto a hook above the television.

"I don't know where to put this bag," she said.

Without a word, Cooper squeezed past her, his thighs rubbing hers, his belt buckle pressing her arm. Lacey felt an odd tingling in her breasts and a fluttering in her stomach and was suddenly very aware of being a woman—and that Cooper was very much a man.

Bending at the knee in order to fit into the compartment, Cooper opened a cabinet above the end of the bed, pulled out two blankets and tossed them beside Jon and Anna, who were sitting on the bed. Then he took the bag from Lacey, placed it into the cabinet and shut the door with a hard snap.

He looked at her, and she looked at him. Realizing that she was in his way, she searched for somewhere to go. The only place was the passenger seat. She sat down immediately.

Cooper took his seat, flipped switches and turned on the headlights. Anna came quietly to wiggle onto Lacey's lap. Lacey held her close and worried if it could possibly harm her children to take this trip with a man who so obviously didn't want them around. What if, at the trip's end, their grandfather did reject them, just as their own father already had? How would that make them feel about themselves?

"Can I watch the television, Mr. Cooper?" Jon called from the back. Obviously Jon wasn't bothered by Cooper's rudeness. But then, Jon could generally return as good as he got.

"Yeah," Cooper said. His hand on the stick shift, he looked at Lacey. "She can't stay here," he said, inclining his head toward Anna. "It's not safe."

Anna gripped Lacey and wasn't about to let go.

"I'll get in the back with her," Lacey said.

Cooper nodded and turned his attention to getting underway. As Lacey cleared the pass-through, the truck gave a gentle jolt of forward motion. Cooper jerked the curtain across the opening, enclosing her and the children in the cozy confines of the sleeper—and himself up front, alone.

Lacey gratefully stretched out beside Anna beneath the bedcovers. She was exhausted and quite chilled. Jon propped himself against her feet, avidly watching a cartoon show, the television providing the only light in the compartment. It was a comfort to have both children physically touching her.

"This is nice," Anna said softly, her eyes wide with wonder. "It's like being rocked."

"Mmm," Lacey answered. For some reason her daughter's innocent fascination touched a raw spot in her heart.

She mused over the idea of spending the entire trip in the sleeping compartment. Surely that would make Mr. Delightful happy. How in the world could Pate think Cooper needed company?

The headlights illuminated the concrete ramp leading down to Interstate 40, and Cooper shifted gears, feeling the big Kenworth easily gain speed. He watched for oncoming vehicles—there was a surprising amount of traffic for so early in the morning. People trying to get home for the holidays, he thought, half bitterly, half wistfully.

The road passed beneath the rig at sixty-five miles an hour. Nearly three days stretched ahead of him before he dropped his load—Pate's load—up in Washington, D.C. He could have made it in less than three if he drove as he usually did. But with the woman and two kids with him, he probably wouldn't.

Cooper turned up the volume of the radio to drown out the murmur of the television. He gave thanks for a foot-stomping Mel McDaniel country tune without a hint of Christmas in it.

Thirty minutes passed, and the sky began to glow with morning. Cooper enjoyed the feeling of the steering wheel in his hands and the smooth rumble of the truck pushing through the wind.

Was that woman going to spend the entire trip back in the sleeper? he wondered. Now that she was here, the least she could do was get up front and fill his coffee cup from his thermos. A fool in a red Corvette pulled dangerously close in front of him, and he let up on the accelerator. He was suddenly very aware of his passengers.

He frowned, thinking of the fear in the little girl's face when she'd looked at him. Was he really so much of a monster? Well, he couldn't pretend to be something he wasn't. He was thirty-eight years old, a bachelor for all intents and purposes, no kids, and he didn't much like them. They reminded him of Martians, a little species with customs and language all their own.

He began to sing along faintly with the radio. The cab didn't seem so empty then.

Minutes later Lacey parted the curtain behind him. He met her gaze in the mirror and stopped his singing. She smiled. She had a rare kind of smile that lit up her entire face and reached out to touch a person. Cooper wanted to smile in return—only he didn't. He didn't want her to get the idea she was welcome or anything. But he had to admit to himself that he didn't mind looking at her, not at all, and that he felt a certain lightness all of a sudden.

Without invitation, she slipped into the passenger seat. Out of the corner of his eye, he noticed her move the armrests up and down, then give a little bounce, like a kid testing the seat.

He stretched out his arm and moved the lever to activate the seat's air cushion. She jumped, and her eyes widened.

"The air," he said, quickly returning his hand to the wheel, "for the seat." What did she think—that he was trying to cop a feel?

He returned his strict attention to the road ahead. It felt odd to have her beside him. He'd never had a woman in his rig, had always purposely avoided it.

Lacey didn't realize she was studying Cooper until he glanced over at her. Self-conscious, she jerked her head to look out the side window and folded her hands in her lap. She wasn't nervous, she told herself, and she didn't care what Cooper thought of her. There was no reason to.

It was cozy in the cab. The change in the seat when he'd moved that lever had surprised her. And now it was like an easy chair at home, though it rocked a bit more. She loved the lordly height of the truck. They passed a Toyota, and she looked down to see the driver's knees, which seemed an intimate observation.

The eastern horizon stretched orange. The shadowy woods and pastures they passed showed signs of heavy frost.

"Looks like a sunny day," Lacey commented. She loved sunny mornings.

"Radio says clouds," Cooper said.

"Oh."

On spying a slowly pumping oil well draped with colorful Christmas lights, she felt a pleasurable warmth flash within her.

"Look! Aren't they pretty?" she cried before she thought. She glanced at Cooper, and he grunted, keeping his eyes on the road.

A man of few words, Lacey thought, feeling self-conscious and childish—and irritable because of it.

He pushed in the lighter, pulled a cigarette from his shirt pocket and tucked it between his lips. For all the attention he paid her, she might as well not be there. Lacey's irritation grew.

Well, they had hours and hours ahead of them, she told herself. Jolene had said Cooper had a softer side, and Pate had said Cooper needed people at this time of year. Maybe he was just sour and distant because he was shy. She could try harder to extend a friendly hand.

"What's a Jacob's Brake?" she asked.

Cooper gave her a lazy glance. "What?" he drawled.

"That." She pointed to the switch labeled with the odd name.

"A brake's all," he said. "I got a lot of wheels to stop." He jerked his thumb back toward the trailer.

Obviously it was something he felt that she, a woman, wouldn't understand. Lacey took a deep breath and pushed away her irritation.

"I had no idea these trucks were like this," she said brightly. "So luxurious. It's really a work of art."

He grunted around his cigarette.

Lacey refused to give up. There'd been few people in her life she couldn't relate to, make friends with. All it took was being friendly first, and that didn't cost much.

She continued to ask questions, and he answered—with one-and two-word sentences or the familiar grunt.

He was hauling computer printers for Pate. He'd known
Pate for twenty years. He lived not far from Pate in
Santa Fe. When he showed no inclination to continue
polite conversation, Lacey fell to silently staring out the
window.

For some unfathomable reason, she wanted to smack
him. Didn't he know that no one liked being treated as
if they were less than a speck on the windshield?

Face it, she told herself baldly, you're miffed because he doesn't take notice of you. You want him to
treat you like a pretty—even desirable?—woman.

"Would you pour me some coffee?" His voice startled her. He handed her the cup from the nearby holder.
"The thermos is right behind my seat," he said.

"Oh..." She smiled. "Sure." So the silent man had
finally spoken—and had asked for something, no less.
She filled his cup with hot coffee, replaced the thermos
and handed him the cup, along with a smile. He didn't
smile in return.

"Thanks," he said, and retreated back into his own
world.

The only sounds in the cab for the next fifteen minutes were the engine's low rumble and music from the
radio. When there came a loud, crackling static and a
man's voice calling out for the Snappy Maroon Kenworth, Lacey jumped. The call came again. "Got your
ears on, Kenworth?"

She listened in fascination as Cooper spoke into the
CB radio microphone and identified himself as the
Solitary Man. He exchanged information with the un-
seen driver, who was heading west, about conditions on
the interstate. Lacey heard some terms she understood,
some that baffled her. "Bear in the air" which meant
police in a plane; "pedal to the metal" which meant

going as fast as possible; something about a "rocking chair heading west," which she didn't understand. Then "five byebye," as a sign-off.

Cooper had actually carried on a friendly conversation—with a total stranger. Something he apparently didn't want to do with her.

Jon poked a bright face around the curtain and said he was hungry. Cooper gave his familiar grunt. Lacey dug into her tote bag and handed Jon a snack cake.

"You know, the danger of cancer is about tripled for passive smokers," Jon said, waving at Cooper's cigarette smoke.

"Then sit in the back so you won't suffer," Cooper drawled.

Lacey vowed to curtail her son's television news watching and had the urge to stuff a sock in his mouth. Lord, how she hated discord in any form. She avoided it religiously; even her divorce had been amicable. Yet never had she been in such close contact with a person who plain didn't like her. It hurt and confused her.

"Mama, I have to go to the bathroom." Anna's young voice squeaked as she poked a sleepy-eyed face beside Jon's.

Cooper turned to Lacey and looked as if he wanted to scream. Very quietly he said, "There's a rest stop up the road about ten minutes."

"That will be fine," she said, equally quietly.

A little past nine o'clock Cooper stopped at a familiar truck stop for breakfast and refueling. Lacey and her kids went on ahead to the restaurant, while he lagged behind to give his brakes a thorough inspection. They'd been performing okay, but he'd sensed something not quite right.

Besides, he'd just as soon be on his own for a few minutes. Nothing in his deal with Pate said he'd have to do anything but give these people a ride; he didn't have to eat with them.

After the inspection revealed nothing amiss with the brakes, Cooper headed for the restaurant, his stomach anticipating a plate of ham and eggs and a cup of scalding black coffee.

The restaurant's entryway was strategically placed right through the trucker's store, and a display of the latest in compact disc players for vehicles drew Cooper's attention. He paused to look at one.

"Pretty slick machine," came a voice from beside him. "Maybe Santa will leave one in your stocking."

Recognizing the smart tone of voice, Cooper slowly turned his head to see the kid, Jon, at his elbow. He'd slicked his light brown hair back from his face and had his hands stuffed into his fashionably baggy denims.

"Listen, kid," Cooper said, feeling an unexplainable annoyance. "You have to work for what you want in this life. There's no free ride. I learned it by the age of five—there is no Santa Claus."

The boy's easy grin seemed to melt and slide right off his face. Shifting his gaze, Cooper experienced a sinking feeling. Peeking around the boy's side was his sister. Her lower lip trembled.

"Anna... Jon." Lacey appeared from the nearby ladies' room doorway. Her gaze moved quickly from the children to Cooper and back again. The little one, Anna, ran to clutch her around the leg.

Cooper looked down at little Anna, who was looking at him as if he had horns again. He'd never felt so completely in over his head; he had no idea what to do.

"Better get some breakfast 'cause I'm leaving here in thirty-five minutes," he said, making an immediate retreat toward the dining room.

Puzzled, Lacey watched Cooper walk away. She looked down at Anna.

"Mama," Anna said, her lower lip trembling as she tightened her grip around Lacey's leg, "he said there's no Santa Claus."

Oh, no, Lacey thought. "I'm sure he didn't mean exactly that, Anna."

"He said it," Anna pronounced logically.

"Aw, Anna," Jon said, "you know some people like to say stuff like that. Cooper, he don't know. He's just like that Scrooge guy in the movie we saw. He can't enjoy Christmas. Now, come on—I'm starved."

Anna went along quietly, and throughout the meal Lacey could practically see the thoughts revolving in her young daughter's mind. Though Lacey considered it cowardly on her part, she was terribly glad Anna didn't ask her straight out about Santa, because she didn't want to tell her daughter the stark truth. Not one bit. She wanted her daughter to hold the magic as long as possible.

Cooper ate alone at the bar, and Lacey found it distinctly awkward. How odd it felt to look at him across the room and know they were traveling in the same vehicle but weren't friendly enough to eat together. And she wasn't friendly enough even to ask him his whole name. Did they *have* to be friends for her to ask that?

It wasn't going to work, Lacey thought starkly as she helped Anna blow her nose. The situation wasn't fair to the children, nor to Cooper. And she didn't think she could remain all sweetness and light for the remainder of the trip, not to mention coming back. Her mind leaped ahead, counting money as usual. She could just barely swing it, though she might need to borrow some money from Beth in case of emergency. She and the children could return to Albuquerque by bus. It was the best way, the only way.

As they finished their meal, Jon talked about Christmases past and the favorite things Santa had brought him, and Lacey sent her very verbal son a grateful smile. He was doing it because he loved his sister.

Later Anna and Lacey were alone in the truck while Cooper saw to the refueling and Jon followed at his heels. Though Lacey knew Cooper probably didn't appreciate it, she didn't forbid Jon; he needed an outlet for his boundless energy.

"Mama, why is Cooper so grumpy?" Anna asked.

Lacey sighed. "I'm not certain, honey. A lot of times a person gets like that from sad things that have happened in his life." She frowned. "Then again, some people are just born grumpy."

"Maybe he doesn't believe in Santa Claus because Santa doesn't bring him anything—because he's too grumpy all the time," Anna said.

"Oh, Santa brings everyone presents, but maybe Cooper just can't see them."

Anna gave a puzzled frown. "That's one of those things I'll understand when I'm older, right?"

Lacey laughed and hugged her. "Right."

Thirty minutes later Lacey told Cooper her intention to make the return trip by bus. She expected her announcement to put him at ease. After all, he could look forward to having them out of his hair.

He didn't smile. "Pate said the trip was both ways."

"I think returning by bus will work out better," she said.

He shrugged. "Suit yourself."

The miles rolled along beneath the massive Kenworth wheels, and they pushed on across the Texas panhandle. Anna had just required her second rest stop in two hours, and Lacey was handing each of the children a juice drink she'd purchased from a machine when Cooper took the cans right out of her hands.

"If we continue to make every rest stop between here and North Carolina, we won't get there till Easter," he said.

"When are we going to get some lunch?" Jon asked. "I'm hungry."

"We don't get lunch," Cooper said. "We'll eat dinner tonight when we stop."

Lacey swiftly reached out and retrieved the drink cans from Cooper. "If you're not planning to stop for lunch, these children need something to drink." She fixed her eyes on him and silently dared him to argue. He didn't.

Reminded ten minutes later by Jon about a growing boy's hunger, Lacey produced homemade cookies and pumpkin bread from her tote bag. As she passed the sweets back to the children, she considered offering some to Cooper. But *he* was the one who'd refused to stop for lunch, she thought smartly. Let him smell the goodies and drool. Minutes later she was shamed by her own six-year-old daughter.

"Mr. Cooper, would you like some of my cookies?" Anna asked in a hesitant voice as she extended two cookies as far toward Cooper as she dared.

Cooper amazed Lacey by taking the cookies and thanking Anna politely.

He likes sweets, Lacey thought, watching him out of the corner of her eye. When he'd finished the cookies, she offered him a slice of the pumpkin bread, feeling almost as if she were offering a bribe. No, she thought as he took the sweet bread, a distinctly sheepish expression on his face. She was trying to build a bridge.

Gray clouds closed in as the afternoon wore on. Cooper learned from fellow truckers on the CB that north of them a storm was wreaking havoc, covering everything with a thick layer of ice and dumping snow in the mountains. So far it looked as if the storm would stay to the north; he hoped so.

The kids retired again to the sleeper compartment. "Napping," Lacey said tersely. Though she sat up front in the cab, she said little and didn't have that friendly air she normally did.

He guessed he couldn't blame her. He had been anything but polite. Before, when she'd said she and the kids would return to Albuquerque by bus, he'd been half relieved, half angry. Now he had this foolish feeling of disappointment and the urge to make friends.

"You going to see your folks in North Carolina?" he asked.

She looked surprised at the question, then pleased. She nodded. "Yes, the children have never met my parents." Lord, her eyes were green. And shimmery.

The silence seemed awfully loud. As he searched for something to say—because he suddenly wanted to talk to her—Cooper had the oddest sensation of being aware of Lacey's breasts gently moving as she breathed.

"Cooper?" Lacey wondered if she really wanted to ask him.

"Yeah?" The interest in his tone gave her courage.

"Is Cooper your first name, your last or what?"

His lips split into a wide grin, his teeth a startling white beneath his dark mustache as he chuckled. "You been wondering about that, have you?"

"Yes, I have."

"Barry B. Cooper is the name."

He sent her a long glance. His eyes twinkled, then changed, as if he was looking deep into her soul. Heat flashed up from the feminine recesses of Lacey's body and filled her cheeks. He seemed, wonder of wonders, to like what he was looking at.

"Nice to meet you, Barry."

"Call me Cooper. I hate Barry."

They'd made an unspoken truce, and gradually that truce mellowed into companionable conversation. Lacey told Cooper she'd been divorced four years and that she hadn't seen her parents since before Jon was born. The main reason for the trip was for the kids to meet their grandparents. They talked of Gerald's restaurant, and Cooper said he'd been stopping there somewhere around ten years; he'd begun driving a truck twenty years before, at the age of eighteen. He'd known Pate almost that long and mentioned "owing the old man," which Lacey interpreted as his reason for giving her and the children a ride.

He was originally from Texas, a million years ago, and had been married once, about that long ago, too. He was also divorced.

Lacey wanted to ask about his family, but an inner instinct kept her quiet. Listening to him, she had a glimpse of a very lonely man, and she saw a reflection of her own well-deep loneliness. It was like that for a lot of people, she thought sadly.

The tires hummed along the highway, soft country music played in the background and they talked of baseball, thick pizzas and dog breeds. Lacey looked at Cooper's profile, which resembled sculpted bronze. She watched his capable hands caress and maneuver the steering wheel and imagined what those hands would feel like on her body. In a flash of keen awareness, she realized she hadn't thought of a man in such a way since well before Shawn had left.

Then she found herself staring into his dark eyes. And she had the uncomfortable inkling that he knew exactly what she'd been thinking. Had perhaps been thinking along the same lines himself.

They were one third of the way across Oklahoma when they stopped for dinner, and this time Cooper sat with them. He appeared only mildly ill at ease as he sat across the table from Lacey. Every time he looked at her, Lacey felt a jangling sensation.

Jon and Cooper actually carried on a conversation about engines and racing, and things seemed to be going great for the first time since they'd started out that morning—until Anna spilled her cola down the back of a man in the adjoining booth. She had been trying to move across the seat on her knees while carrying her glass. She'd bumped her elbow, sloshing the crushed ice and cold liquid in a neat arc through the air and down the man's collar.

The man let out a resounding holler. "What the hell!"

Lacey's waitressing instincts set her to grabbing napkins from the stubborn dispenser that insisted on hanging on to them. "Oh, I'm so sorry," she said when at last she could hand the man a wad. She extended them, then let her hand drop as the man rose from the booth, shaking the back of his shirt.

She found herself looking up into the face of a crazed red-haired giant, who was bellowing words fit only for ships at sea. Anna cowered behind Lacey's leg, sobbing. Then a hand pressed Lacey's shoulder, and she found herself being pushed aside, Cooper's taut back coming between her and the giant.

"That's enough." Cooper's command cut the air. "It was an accident." Having to look up at the red-haired man didn't seem to bother him. "You owe these ladies an apology."

"Me?" The man clamped his jaw tightly, then glanced around the restaurant, seeing all the faces staring at him. A final look at Cooper must have decided him. "My...apologies, ladies," he muttered, squeezing back into his seat and hunching his massive shoulders in disgust.

Cooper lifted a wide-eyed Anna into his arms and carried her grandly from the dining room. "Stop in the bathroom," he said in the lobby as he lowered the little girl to the floor.

"Cooper—" Lacey began, but Cooper interrupted.

"Go on. I don't want to have to stop again ten minutes down the road."

Chapter Four

Cooper blamed his preoccupation with both the truck's brakes and Lacey Bryant for his overlooking the good probability that the red-haired hulk would come after him, seeking satisfaction for the small fracas in the restaurant. If Cooper had been thinking at all, he told himself, he would have been ready and waiting.

As it was, he was bending over near the trailer, checking the cables and tires, when he heard the man's shout. He barely had time to straighten and get a bead on the guy before the man swung, his fist plowing neatly into Cooper's cheek.

It didn't last long, and Cooper got in a few licks of his own before the hulk sent one final blow that knocked Cooper to the ground. Satisfied, the man hitched up his pants and lumbered away.

Cooper was picking himself up from the blacktop when he heard Lacey's voice and running footsteps. "Cooper? What—"

He quickly tried to straighten his shoulders, though it hurt like hell. Tentatively, he felt the already swelling skin beneath his left eye. He licked blood from the corner of his mouth.

"Oh, Lord..." Lacey, hovering, pressed a tissue to his cheek. Her womanly warmth drifted out and around him. He enjoyed her ministrations for a brief moment, then came to himself and pulled away.

"It was that big guy from the restaurant, wasn't it, Coop?" Jon said. "How'd you do?"

"Well, he doesn't look too good, either," Cooper said, taking the fresh tissue Lacey handed him and pressing it to a small cut beside his eye. He wasn't about to tell the kid, or Lacey, that about the best he'd done was give the hulk a split lip. "Let's get into the truck."

"Cooper, maybe we should go to the hospital...."

"Aw, Mom, Cooper don't need no doctor," Jon said.

"Just get in the truck, Lacey." Cooper jerked open the driver's side door and hoisted himself up, leaving her standing there. She moved around to her own side.

When Anna passed through to the sleeper, she touched his shoulder. Her brown eyes were large and wet. "I'm sorry, Cooper."

"It's okay, kid." He winked with his good eye. "Everybody has accidents." Then he turned quickly away. No one had cared about his welfare for over fifteen years, and it made him feel as uncomfortable and confused as a bear walking down a city street to see the kind of looks these three people were giving him.

Cooper wasn't about to say he hurt all over, but Lacey saw it—in the way he shifted in his seat to find the most comfortable position, the fleeting wince when he stretched to flip the switches.

She remained quiet. It seemed the safest, wisest course. She felt terrible. It was because of her that Cooper was probably having the worst trip of his entire life. And now, because of her, he'd had his life endangered and was in pain with a hideous swollen eye.

They continued across Oklahoma, through several long sections of cold rain, and stopped for the night at a motel just off the interstate in Henryetta. The clerk assumed they were all together, husband and wife and children. Confusion ensued when Lacey and Cooper, talking at once, with interjections by Jon, tried to explain.

"You want a separate room for the children?" the clerk asked when he could get a word in.

"For the three of them." Cooper pointed at Lacey and the kids.

The clerk shot her a questioning look. Lacey nodded and watched the man's gaze move rapidly from herself to the children to Cooper and settle curiously on Cooper's black eye.

"You got it now?" Cooper said sharply enough that Anna jumped.

"Yes, sir." The clerk lowered his gaze and fiddled beneath the counter. "Just sign in here, ma'am. Room number 54." He slid the key across the counter. "Here you are, sir. Room 55." He appeared thoroughly pleased with himself.

Lacey marched the children down the row of rooms to theirs, which was second from the end. The last one was Cooper's. Right next to theirs.

She unlocked the door for the children, then went to the truck to get their bags. Five minutes later she found herself standing in front of her room, Cooper beside her, in front of his room. For some reason she couldn't understand in the least, it was a very awkward moment.

Cooper twisted his key; Lacey pushed open her door, which had been left ajar. They paused and looked at each other. The flesh surrounding Cooper's left eye was the color of roiling thunder clouds.

"I'm so sorry about what happened," Lacey said. "Does it hurt terribly?"

Cooper took a deep breath. "It hurts—but I'll live."
His dark eyes searched hers, as if seeking answers to
something that puzzled him.

"Mama, do I have to take a bath?" Anna called, her
voice bursting into the moment.

"Good night," Lacey said to Cooper, her gaze still
riveted by his. What were the questions? She had them,
too, yet she didn't know what they were.

"Good night."

Then they each entered their own rooms. The two
doors clicked closed at the same time.

Needing time alone, Lacey got Jon and Anna into
bed before taking her shower. After having risen so
early, the children fell asleep as soon as they'd settled
who got which pillow. The ensuing silence was more
than golden; it was heaven to Lacey.

As she leisurely undressed she could hear the muffled sound of the television in Cooper's room. She
wondered what he was watching.

Was he a late-night or early-morning person? Did he
like showers or baths? She continued to wonder as she
stood beneath the massaging heat of steaming water.
Would he think she had a good body?

Just as she'd turned off the water, she heard a peculiar knocking. Someone rapping on the wall, she realized as she stood in the tub, rivulets of water running
down her skin. Cooper? Knocking out a rhythm on the
wall?

Lacey hesitated only one self-conscious second,
wondering if indeed Cooper was knocking on purpose
or if perhaps it came from something he was doing.
Throwing caution to the winds, she rapped back, imi-
tating his rhythm. She held her breath.

It came again. Cooper had knocked in return!

Lacey clamped a hand over her mouth, stifling her laughter for fear of waking the children and having to answer for her actions. But it was hilariously funny. Two grown people engaging in a childish stunt. She couldn't believe Cooper would do such a thing. Not solemn, gruff Cooper, who'd spent most of the day treating her as if she wasn't there.

She knocked again and waited expectantly, but no more knocks came. Only silence.

With a sigh, Lacey pulled a plush towel from the nearby rack and began drying herself. She was suddenly exhausted, and very lonely. When she crawled into the big double bed, she pulled the extra pillow into her arms and held it tight.

Morning came much too early. Immediately upon turning off the alarm, Lacey discovered that the rumbling she heard was the Kenworth engine—already running. How revolting. It was still pitch black, for heaven's sake.

Allowing the children a few minutes' extra sleep, she ran across the parking lot to the large gas station–minimart to get sweet rolls and milk to tide them over until breakfast. At the last minute, she bought a sweet roll for Cooper, too.

Cooper knocked at their door while Jon was still dressing. "Come on, let's go." He definitely sounded testy.

Lacey didn't bother to awaken Anna enough for her to dress but gathered her up in her arms and carried her to the truck. Without speaking, Cooper helped get Anna into the sleeper in the back, then slipped into the driver's seat, leaving Lacey and Jon to cope with their baggage.

When he shifted the truck into gear without as much as a "good morning," Lacey wondered if the knocking she'd heard the night before had happened at all. Perhaps she'd imagined it. When he switched off the radio in the middle of "Santa Claus Is Coming to Town," Lacey figured she had the answer to the question of whether he was a morning person or not. And when he snapped at her to please stop that noise, calling her attention to the fact she was now unconsciously humming "Santa Claus Is Coming to Town," she called herself a saint for buying a dyed-in-the-wool Scrooge a sweet roll.

She gave him the roll, however, with every ounce of pleasantry she possessed. He scowled—but he took it. Heaven knew he needed all the sweetness he could ingest. And she continued to feel overwhelmingly guilty about his eye, which, while less swollen, remained the color of thunderheads.

Cooper stopped a bit early for breakfast and varied his schedule to stop for lunch, too. He didn't know much about kids, but he knew enough about people to tell when two young ones were restless enough to explode. He was experiencing something similar himself. The feelings were unfamiliar and damned annoying. Never had he felt so keenly that he wanted to be anywhere but in the truck, stuck in one position behind the wheel.

He hadn't slept well. His face and various bruised parts of his body had throbbed. And he'd kept thinking about Lacey. She was causing him no end of discomfort. Her green eyes were warm and full to bursting with life. Her scent drew him like a magnet. He couldn't seem to quit sneaking peeks at her body—her sleek thighs hugged by blue denim, her breasts full and round beneath her soft sweater, her creamy neck and chin. Last night he'd imagined what she looked like in the shower, just on the other side of the wall. He'd wanted, for some really weird reason, to communicate with her. After he'd knocked, he'd felt a fool. But it was pleasing that she'd knocked in return.

Lord, she must think him some kind of nut. And he *knew* he was having thoughts he shouldn't be having. Besides the practical side, there was Pate to consider.

"I'm going to go ahead and see about fuel," he told Lacey, leaving the steakburger he'd ordered only half finished. "I'll meet you and the kids at the truck."

He simply couldn't sit still. Besides, he told himself, he was falling further and further behind schedule all the time. Several rest stops this morning, now lunch. Good grief! They'd be lucky to get to North Carolina before the new year.

After paying for the fuel he was stuffing bills into his wallet when he looked through the station window into the small gift shop beyond. The kid, Jon, stood there examining something on a glass shelf—when he was supposed to have his butt out at the truck.

Cooper strode around the pumps and entered the store. "Come on, kid. This isn't a sight-seeing tour, you know." Something in the boy's expression stopped him. Taking another step forward, Cooper glanced down to see a woman's fancy brush-and-comb set on the glass display shelf. He took a second look at the boy.

"I was thinking of getting it for Mom," the kid said. "For Christmas."

"Well, get it and let's go."

Jon shuffled toward the door. "I'm goin'."

"Hey, you can take a minute to get this if you want."

The kid scuffed his feet. "Naw. I'm a bit short, and she probably wouldn't like it anyway."

Though he acted as if it were of little importance, Cooper suspected otherwise. The kid wanted to get this for Lacey.

"How much short are you?" Cooper asked, pulling out his wallet.

"Six dollars."

"Here." Cooper extended a ten. "I'll advance you this, if you make certain my windshield's clean at every stop and be my general gofer, handling whatever I tell you."

The kid eyed the money, then cast Cooper a suspicious look. "Whatever you tell me?"

"I'm not a slave-driver, if that's what's worrying you. Now, do you want the money or not?"

The kid hesitated only an instant. "You bet!" He snatched the bill and reached for the brush-and-comb set. "I'll be out in just a minute." He'd lit up like fireworks on the Fourth of July—and an unusual warmth spread within Cooper as well.

"What is it?" Lacey asked when he reached the truck several minutes later.

Only then did Cooper realize he was smiling, and for almost no reason. "Oh, nothin'...." He looked at her for several long seconds, and she looked back. Slowly that special smile of hers broke across her face, and Cooper recognized then the one thing that made Lacey Bryant unique. She could smile and laugh over nothing at all.

Lacey knew something had transpired between Cooper and Jon. Jon returned to the truck with a secret smile for Cooper and a bag he immediately hid. Her

Christmas present, she guessed. But where did Cooper fit into it? And why was he suddenly smiling, too?

She decided whatever had gone on between the two was definitely welcome, because a mellow atmosphere seemed to permeate the cab. Cooper didn't turn off the Christmas carols when they came on the radio, and he didn't even scowl when Jon and Anna began singing along with "Jingle Bells." Lacey dared to join in, and, lo and behold, Cooper shot them all what could have passed for a grin—at least for him. The next song was "Joy to the World," and they sang that, too, then listened attentively to the weather report. A winter storm was pushing down from the north. Though it didn't look as if it would make it into the states of Arkansas and Tennessee, there was a chance.

"We'll make it to Grandpa's and Grandma's by Christmas Eve, won't we?" Anna asked Cooper, her eyebrows furrowed. "I have to be there to get the puppy Santa's bringing me."

"We'll get there for Christmas Eve, darling," Lacey said quickly.

"Santa's bringing me a puppy," Anna said to Cooper. When he didn't reply, she said, "Cooper, didn't Santa bring you presents when you were a kid?"

Lacey sucked in a breath and sent Cooper a silent warning. He glanced quickly at Anna by way of his rearview mirror, then looked at the road.

"I can't remember that he did," he said slowly. Lacey wondered at his words, at the dead way he said them. It didn't take a lot of imagination to guess his childhood had been bleak.

"You said you didn't believe in him," Anna said quietly.

Cooper looked at a loss—and quite annoyed. "I guess I don't.

"Maybe that's why you never got anything," Anna said.

"Maybe so." Cooper dug into his pocket for a cigarette.

"Anna, that's enough," Lacey said. "You and Jon get in back and take a nap.

They did as she said, though Jon protested all the way. But they were tired from two days of early rising, and even Jon fell asleep within fifteen minutes. Lacey watched the scenery roll past and noted the darkening skies.

"Guess your parents are anxious about you coming," Cooper said after a few minutes, making a surprising attempt at conversation. "They probably weren't real thrilled with how you and the kids are getting there."

"They don't know we're coming," Lacey said. At his raised eyebrow, she continued. "It's a surprise—a ploy, really. You see, my father and I haven't spoken in eleven years." She went on to tell the entire story of being unwed and pregnant, and of her father's fury, her own resentment. "I'd always been the problem child. My getting pregnant was just the last straw, so to speak."

"The man's held his peace for eleven years. What if he doesn't bend now?" Cooper asked, obviously skeptical of her methods. "Where will you stay?"

"With my sister."

"And what about the kids? How do you think they'll feel if their own grandpa turns them away?" He fired the questions at her.

"I admit, I'm taking a chance," Lacey said, feeling the need to defend herself. "But I really think my father will not only bend but melt when he sees his grandchildren.''

"Maybe..." Cooper lit a cigarette and fell into thought. "My mother left me with my grandparents," he said quietly. "They didn't want to be saddled with a six-year-old kid, so they took me to the orphanage—we had them in those days. I bounced around in foster homes, too. Finally, at fifteen, I went back to see my grandpa. He told me they didn't have room for me."

Lacey watched the pain flicker across his profile before it was swallowed up in a calculated blank expression.

"My father and I fought," she said finally, "terribly. But he loved me. And that was the cause of his anger—not uncaring." She paused. "Not everyone in your life could have been like your grandparents."

He shook his head slightly. "They weren't."

"Then why don't you forget them and let yourself enjoy Christmas?"

He gave a harsh chuckle. "I forgot them a long time ago. And Christmas is just a time for a lot of people to make money."

The bitterness in his words took her breath away, and she spoke before she thought.

"Oh, how can you say that? Why, even the most hardened of criminals feels love in his heart at this time of year. Wars have stopped at Christmas," she said, as if that were undeniable proof of her stand. She gestured. "Sure, there's Christmas hype, but only because people enjoy it so much—you know, giving the customer what he wants. Christmas is a time when people can enjoy pure, unadulterated loving without feeling embarrassed or threatened."

"You ought to take off those rose-colored glasses," Cooper said with scorn. "What people call love is just lumps of fears and selfish motives in disguise."

Lacey had never met anyone like Cooper. "You don't believe in Santa Claus, you don't believe in Christmas and you don't believe in love. What do you believe in, Barry Cooper?"

"Myself," he said flatly. "And don't call me Barry."

Lacey felt sorry for him, very sorry. But of course she couldn't say such a thing, and she turned away quickly so he wouldn't see the pity on her face. The devil of it, she thought, was that underneath, just like Jolene and Pate had said, Cooper had a soft spot crying out to love and be loved.

Why did he have to be so contrary? She wanted to like him. She wanted... Oh, she thought darkly, cutting off further imaginings in that direction, they were only foolish impossibilities.

Cooper glanced at Lacey. Her hands lay loosely in her lap; she looked very small. And as if she'd been dealt a big blow. Cooper felt he'd been a bit harsh with his words. Yet he'd been truthful.

She really believed in all those forgiving and forgetting and loving fantasies. He hoped she didn't get to Pine Grove and suffer a rude awakening. He hoped doubly so for the kids. The thought that Lacey's father might turn them all away made him flinch. He didn't want them to suffer that. Suddenly he felt an overwhelming sense of protectiveness. He'd punch the man, old or not, if the guy didn't do right by Lacey and those kids.

When he realized his thoughts, he almost stopped breathing. What business was it of his? What did he care if Lacey lived in a fantasy world? *It wasn't any of his business.*

Traffic thickened the closer they came to Nashville, and it seemed a goodly number of fools were trying to kill themselves by pulling over in front of Cooper's Kenworth. Again he had the sense of trouble with the brakes, and this sense was confirmed when they locked on him for several seconds. Ten miles farther down the road, he pulled off the interstate to a familiar truck-stop-and-motel complex on the outskirts of the city.

Cooper was out and around to Lacey's side of the truck, checking tires as he went, before she made it out of her seat. When her door swung open, it seemed the natural thing to raise his arms and help her down.

His hands slipped up beneath her short coat and closed around her waist. It was warm. She pressed her hands to his shoulders for balance, and Cooper lowered her slowly. A sweet fragrance floated from her hair. Then her thighs were brushing his, and he was looking into her eyes.

"Thank you," she said softly.

"Sure."

A movement from above caught his attention, reminding him that he remained with his hands at Lacey's waist. He jerked them away and looked up at the same time, finding Jon staring down at him with a curious and guarded expression. Cooper had the uncomfortable feeling the kid had read his mind.

"I'll follow you in a few minutes," he said to Lacey, keeping his gaze on his pack of cigarettes. "I want to see if a mechanic here can take a look at the brakes."

"There's a problem?" she asked, her voice breathless.

He glanced up to see her keeping silken strands of hair from blowing into her eyes. He shook his head. "Just a small one. Nothing to worry about." He turned, feeling her gaze on him as he walked quickly away.

Though the mechanic corrected the problem with the brakes in short order, causing no delay, after dinner Cooper elected to stay in the nearby motel. It was a neat, clean place, yet very inexpensive, which he knew would be a help to Lacey. From a couple of remarks she'd made, he knew she supported her kids alone, without any help from her ex-husband. Ordinarily on a haul like this, Cooper would have spent every other night in his truck, but riding with Lacey, he preferred to get a shower and not appear so rumpled.

"What about the storm?" she asked him over their coffee. "Several people here have said it isn't looking good."

Cooper nodded. "Driver over at the garage said up north the highways were closing. But it hasn't turned south yet, and it may not. No sense worrying about it beforehand, but I'll keep a watch, and if the storm looks like it has turned this way, I'll get you and the kids."

This time the room he was given was four doors away from Lacey's. They were lucky to get rooms at all with the heavy holiday traffic.

When Lacey had said her good-night and closed the door, Cooper experienced the oddest sensation of abandonment.

His room was immaculate and modernly stark—bed, dresser, small portable television. He tossed his coat onto the bed, then turned on the television. Absently he watched *The Beverly Hillbillies* and smoked a cigarette. Then he examined his face in the mirror. His eye looked a bit better now, he thought, though he couldn't swear to it. It didn't hurt so much anyway. Lacey must have gotten used to it, because around lunchtime she'd quit getting that expression of guilt every time she looked at him. She'd smiled a lot during dinner.

He'd bet she was having some of the same thoughts he was having, and he didn't think the assumption was all ego on his part. If they'd been alone on this trip, Cooper wondered if he'd be in this room right now—or down in hers.

Stupid thought! he raged at himself. She wasn't a woman to fool around with under any circumstances. And there was Pate to consider.

Suddenly Cooper didn't want to be in the room another minute. Grabbing his coat, he headed out the door and strode along the road toward the shopping center that was just across the highway overpass. The wind was sharp, and passing cars made it sharper. It felt good to be out in the open.

At a discount department store, where he'd come for a carton of cigarettes, Cooper found himself musing over an array of stuffed animals. He chose a wrinkled puppy with a vest and bow tie for Anna. It didn't cost all that much, he told himself.

But of course he couldn't buy that and not get something for Jon, so he wandered over to the toy section. It was bleak, with most of the toys sold out. Unwilling to give up, he meandered back through the boys' clothing department and spied a bright red jacket with black Corvette insignias on it. Guessing at size, he picked one and headed for the checkout counter before he could do anything else foolish. He'd left the store before he realized he'd forgotten his cigarettes and had to return for them.

On his way out of the mall, he glanced into a gift shop window and spied a crystal-ball snow scene. The ball was a bit larger than his gear-shift knob, sat atop stained oak and had a miniature Christmas tree inside. After only a second's hesitation, he went in to buy it. Lacey might like it, he thought. It was something, anyway.

He headed back to the motel. When he entered his room, he set his packages on the bed and wondered what in the world had gotten into him.

Well, he told himself, he hadn't gone out of his way. He'd been at the stores; he'd had the money. Probably the kids would enjoy some extra things. Couldn't get kids too many gifts.

Lacey had said she would return to Albuquerque by bus, and she probably couldn't afford it. Well, he thought almost angrily, she was an adult. She knew what she was doing.

Still restless, Cooper watched television for the weather report, then walked outside and down the row of rooms to the soft-drink machine at the middle of the building. He saw light showing at the edges of the heavy drapes as he passed Lacey's room. Was she up, or had she just left the light on?

On his way back, cold soft-drink can in hand, Cooper stopped in front of Lacey's door. He had the oddest feeling of certainty and uncertainty warring within him. The image of the stark room waiting for him flashed through his mind. The next instant, almost without choosing, he raised his hand and knocked softly.

He immediately thought he needed to have his head examined and was about to walk away when the curtains moved and Lacey peered out at him. Then the curtains fell back into place. He heard her fiddling with the lock, and anticipation mixed with the impulse to run. He'd never felt so screwed up.

The door opened, and Lacey stood silhouetted against the soft light from the room.

"Hi," she said.

"Hi."

She was still dressed, her hair fluffy, like she'd been running her hands through it. She stepped forward and quietly pulled the door closed behind her.

Chapter Five

"Kids asleep?" Cooper asked.

Lacey nodded. "They were exhausted." She folded her arms and hugged herself. The north wind was bitter. "Hear something about the weather?"

Cooper looked puzzled, then understanding dawned. He shook his head. "Oh, no...no." He raised the can in his hand. "I'd just come out for this."

Though she couldn't clearly see his eyes or assess his expression because of the dim light on the porch, she felt the warmth of him. She told herself it was because he'd shifted to where he blocked the wind. And she scoffed at the idea he could be attracted to her.

Cooper cleared his throat. "Look, Lacey, you'd arranged to ride back to Albuquerque with Pate. I'll be going back just like he would. You and the kids might as well come along."

She had to smile. "Think you could stand the kids?"

"Hey, it's only a few days," he answered with a hint of a smile.

His eyes were very dark as he stared at her, his smile fading. The wind snatched at his thick hair, and the yellow glow of the porch light magnified the bruise around his eye. Lacey caught the scents of cigarette smoke, leather from his coat and faint male cologne.

His gaze moved from her eyes to her lips, then back up to her eyes again. He leaned very close, and Lacey didn't want him to go away. Attraction, vibrant and undeniable, filled the air.

"Here, take my coat," he said in a husky voice.

Automatically she shook her head. "No...then you'll be without..." But he was already shrugging out of it. "You'll be cold...."

He slipped it around her awkwardly, one hand still holding the soft drink. The back of his hand caressed her neck, and she knew without doubt that he'd done it on purpose. Her breathing became shallow. His gaze never wavered.

"The first time I saw you in Gerald's place four years ago, I wanted to kiss you," he said.

Lacey's heartbeat rushed like water downhill over pebbles. "The first time I saw you, I wanted to touch your cheek to see if you were as cold as you looked."

He gave a guttural chuckle, his black eyes boring into her.

"I didn't want you to come on this trip."

"I know."

"Pate never said... Is there anything between you and him?"

She shook her head. "Not like you're thinking. He's a good friend."

He nodded and seemed to be mulling over her words. "I haven't meant to be an ass—I'm just not good with kids."

"It's okay. I know we came as a big shock to you...."

Her voice drifted off as she looked at him. Slowly she raised her hand to touch his cheek. She felt the stubble of a beard on his warm skin. Heat flooded her, and she forgot the cold wind. She became aware only of his eyes hot upon her and of the deep longings bubbling up and seeping through every cell in her body. He bent close, his arms closing about her, capturing her own arms within his coat.

Then he was kissing her. Hard and demanding, he forced her lips to part. His lips were hot and velvet and magical upon hers. She savored the waves of heat and pulsing energy that washed over her, the sweet weakness in her knees, the warm male smell of him and the strength of his arms supporting her.

It had been so long since she'd been kissed, so long since she had returned a kiss, totally, fully, with no reserve. And it had been a long time since a man had made her feel so completely and wonderfully a woman.

She gasped for breath when he pulled away. Though his face remained shadowed, she knew instinctively his silent questioning. No words were needed, just as she needed no time to decide. But she remained in his embrace, loathe for the wondrous moment to end.

Then slowly, and so gently that a throbbing ache opened up within Lacey, he kissed her again—a kiss of goodbye. He pulled back and looked at her. She wiggled her hand up to touch his cheek one last time. He reached behind her and pushed open the door to her room.

"Good night," he said, breaking away. He gave a lopsided grin, and the familiar coldness came over him.

It was a long moment before Lacey could find her voice and force it past the lump in her throat. "Good night," she managed as she handed him his coat. She turned and entered her room so that she wouldn't see him walk away.

Sleep was next to impossible. Lacey tossed and turned, trying to be rid of the ache of longing that filled her. She clutched the spare pillow but found it a poor substitute for the warm arms of a loving man.

Had he expected her to go to his room with him? She sincerely doubted it. And it was only carnal instinct between them, she thought. They were both lonely. The attraction had always been there between them; now it had a chance to be acknowledged.

To cause them no end of trouble, Lacey thought irritably. She punched her pillow, thinking that he'd certainly been a cold fish when he'd left her. He'd probably had a hundred women react to him the way she had. And right now he was probably sleeping peacefully, having forgotten all about their little encounter. Damn him for that!

Lacey was awakened by a loud pounding on the door. "Lacey...Lacey!" While she struggled to find her way from beneath the covers, she heard the door open and Jon's voice.

Freed at last from the blankets, she stumbled to the open door, finding Cooper filling it. "What time is it?" She had trouble getting her eyes to focus, but she could see it was still black outside. She was tired of getting up before the chickens, and her irritability focused on the man before her.

"Four-fifteen," Cooper said. He allowed his gaze to run up and down Lacey once, seeing the outline of her curves beneath her soft flannel gown. Her eyes were heavy with sleep, her hair like it'd been in a tornado, her cheeks a warm blush. "The storm's turned," he ground out. "It's on its way, and we'd better be on ours if we want to get to Pine Grove by evening."

He turned and slammed the door behind him, retreating to the familiar comfort of the Kenworth. Christmas Eve had arrived, and he was supposed to deliver Lacey and her kids to their family tonight. The sooner, the better, he told himself, munching on a sweet roll.

He hadn't expected her to come with him to his room last night, though, to be honest, maybe he'd hoped. But hell, she couldn't do that—she had the kids to think of. And what was he to her? What was she to him? Nothing.

The way he was thinking was crazy. What had happened to him? He'd barely dozed two hours the previous night. With intimate thoughts of Lacey plaguing him, he'd finally given up on sleep, dressed and returned to the restaurant, downing cups of coffee while he kept an ear out for the road conditions. Thirty minutes ago he'd heard that the storm had not only turned but had picked up fury as it blew across the plains. Within two hours, Interstate 40 to the west across Oklahoma and Texas had been closed because of snow.

And now they had to get on the road or they'd be stuck. Which meant he'd be stranded with Lacey and her two children. And something told him his very life was threatened by that prospect.

Within twenty minutes Lacey had herself and Jon dressed, their bags gathered, and Cooper was helping a sleepy Anna into the sleeper. Cooper had thought to buy coffee, milk and sweet rolls for the early hours, and at eight they stopped just long enough for a quick breakfast and to refuel the truck. It began to snow then, big heavy flakes. East of them icy rain had fallen, coating the road. Behind them snow pushed from the west.

Lacey found it difficult to meet Cooper's eyes and was glad he had to keep sharp attention on the road. Still, her gaze kept straying to his profile, then down to his hands on the wheel, her mind remembering the feel

of his lips on hers. It probably hadn't meant a thing to
him, she told herself. She recalled Jolene's comment:
Cooper wasn't the marrying kind. And he wasn't *her*
kind, either.

Her insides became tighter and tighter as she sat and
watched the outside world grow whiter. When she cautioned the children to be quiet, she had to grit her teeth
to keep from yelling. The worries piled up in her mind.
Would they make Pine Grove by evening? Somehow she
wasn't in as much of a hurry now. She dreaded saying
goodbye to Cooper, even though they'd hardly said five
words to each other all morning. Would her father accept them? Would she be able to borrow enough from
Beth to get them home again? No way could she ride
with Cooper; he'd know how she felt, and she'd feel a
fool. Would Cooper ever be just another customer to
her again?

The traffic thickened in the mountains, as did the
falling snow, piling up inch by inch. Repeatedly Cooper swore under his breath at vehicles pulling in front of
him, slamming on their brakes, slowing dangerously.
He commanded the children to get into the bed of the
sleeper and stay there, and he checked twice to make
certain Lacey had her seat belt buckled.

Just past noon they were forced to leave the highway. It had been closed ahead because of drifting snow,
though it was expected to be cleared within the hour.

"Good a time as any for lunch," Cooper said,
bringing the big truck to a stop in a restaurant parking
lot.

He stretched his arms, and Lacey saw the lines of
strain around his eyes. For a brief moment she dared to
meet his gaze. Surprised, she saw an unusual softness

in his dark eyes as they met hers. An intimate smile, all for her, quirked his lips.

"Are we gonna make it to Grandpa's by Christmas Eve, Cooper?" Anna asked in a worried voice as they trudged through the wet snow to the crowded restaurant.

Cooper paused and looked down at her. "I'll get you there, squirt, if I can at all." In a fluid, surprising motion, he swooped Anna up into his arms. "Let's keep your feet dry. Don't want to make your cold worse on vacation."

When word came that the highway had been opened to eastbound traffic, Cooper turned to Lacey with a raised eyebrow. "We can go, but it's one lane, and it's slick out there. There is danger."

Lacey appreciated Cooper's consideration of her and the children. In fact, his consulting her came as a warm surprise.

"We have to get to Grandpa's, Mama," Anna said. "Or else Santa won't know where we are."

"Cooper can handle it, Mom," Jon said.

She touched her son's arm. "Of course we're going on."

Lacey struggled to peer through the windshield. The wipers thumped rapidly as the Kenworth pushed through the swirling white gloom, and the hard north wind made a muffled roaring sound. The CB radio crackled occasionally; Cooper left it on to listen for word of highway conditions to the east and to pass along information to drivers heading west. Music from the radio provided a low background to it all. Twice, on two different stations, they heard "White Christmas."

The snow was blowing back onto the road faster than the plows could keep it clear. Repeatedly, the truck plunged through drifts that completely obliterated the pavement. Lacey caught occasional glimpses of two other semi rigs up ahead. Directly in front of them was a red station wagon, a blessing to follow with visibility so poor.

Though she could feel the tug of the wind and the frequent sliding of the truck's wheels, she was confident in Cooper. All his attention was focused on his driving, and it was as if he were attached to the truck, anticipating its every movement. And she suspected, by the rapt look on his face, that he secretly loved the challenge of driving in such abominable weather.

It had begun to grow quite dim when it happened. A brownish sedan came pushing around them in a rare wide spot in the road. As Cooper braked slightly and struggled to keep the Kenworth on the road, he said something under his breath that Lacey couldn't make out but knew was foul. The sedan's taillights disappeared immediately into the gloom. Lacey strained to see, expecting to find the sedan nose first in a snowbank on the shoulder, as they'd seen many others.

She glanced to Cooper and saw a worried frown crease his brow. He let out a curse, and Lacey looked again out the windshield to see red lights, taillights, getting rapidly larger.

Cooper reacted immediately, but he had to be careful. Coming down on the brakes too fast could jackknife the trailer and even overturn the entire rig. The red lights seemed to grow larger right in front of his eyes; the damned car ahead was stopped in the middle of the road!

He applied the brakes as hard as he dared. The trailer began to skid back and forth across the narrow strip of road, dragging the truck with it. Then, in frustrating slow motion, despite Cooper's frantic turning of the wheel, the truck left the highway and pushed its way down the sloping ground. It came to rest quietly, snugged all around in snow.

"Lacey...you all right?" Cooper ran his gaze over her, and relief surged through him when she appeared to be only mildly shaken.

She nodded and jerked around. "Anna? Jon?"

Assured that everyone was in one piece, Cooper reached for his coat and, with Jon's eager assistance, got out to have a look. He knew beforehand, though, that there would be no getting the truck up on the road again without help.

Cooper and Jon reentered the cab along with cold wind and swirling snowflakes. Lacey knew at once by Cooper's expression that they were quite stuck. "What about that car in the road? Are they all right?" she asked.

Jon answered. "The stupid car's gone, Mom."

Looking thoroughly disgusted, Cooper reached for the CB radio microphone. The crackling answer came: help would be sent as soon as they could get through. For now, wait.

"I'm hungry, Mom," Jon said.

"I'm cold," Anna said.

"Guess I agree with both," Cooper said, a grin twisting his lips.

Lacey experienced the sudden absurd feeling of being free and happy. They were all safe and comfortable, the truck's engine continued to purr, putting out heat, and Lacey had plenty of sweet rolls and cookies left in her tote bag. And for the first time in over four years she was spending Christmas Eve in the company of a handsome man she'd come to care a lot about.

After they'd all eaten sweet rolls warmed in the microwave, Lacey tucked herself and the children into the warmth of the bed. When Anna began worrying about Santa Claus, Lacey tried to divert her by telling stories about both children when they'd been babies. Soon Anna and then Jon fell asleep. Lacey laid her head back, lulled, and idly looked at Cooper smoking a cigarette up in the driver's seat.

When she noticed him rubbing his arms as if cold, she said, "Might as well join us. There's room." She wriggled herself and Anna over, indicating the empty space at the end of the bed.

Cooper looked at her, then quirked his mouth. "Think I will. We've got a long night ahead."

Lacey leaned toward Anna, trying not to get too familiarly close to Cooper. It was impossible, of course.

Cooper slipped an arm around her shoulder. "It's okay. I promise I'm not a man to take advantage." He stroked her arm lightly with his thumb.

"Oh, no?" She couldn't keep the smile from her lips.

He grinned. "No...at least not in front of witnesses."

After a moment's hesitation, Lacey decided she wasn't a person to *miss* an advantage, so she leaned back into Cooper's offered shoulder. It felt so good. She wondered what he felt, if anything. What was he thinking? His heart beat against her arm, and he was so wonderfully warm. She drifted off into the sweetness of the moment.

Motion and hushed whispers awoke Lacey. She thought she heard jingling. "Mama..." Jon shook her leg. "Santa..." That was Anna. Then Cooper said, "I'll be damned...."

Lacey rubbed her eyes and poked her head around Cooper and Jon to see what everyone was staring at out the passenger-seat window. She saw Santa Claus highlighted in the glow that spilled from the truck. Light snow fell on the red knitted cap on his head.

She blinked, thinking it was a dream.

But the smiling Santa remained. Anna rolled down the window. "Hi, Santa! Hi! Do you have my puppy?"

"Oh, missy, it's too cold out here for a puppy," the Santa said, never missing a beat. Lacey would have bet a month's tips that his beard was real, as was his nearly shoulder-length white hair. His coat was black, but the pants beneath were bright red.

The wind had stopped, and the snow fell softly now. Road crews were working hard, Santa told them, offering them a ride to the Mountain View Lodge up the road about three miles. Oh, he had some time, he assured a most concerned Anna. Several yards away sat Santa's odd-looking wagon-sleigh, pulled by two draft horses, bells jingling on their harness.

Cooper got out first, and for some odd reason he and Santa walked to the back of the trailer. Lacey scrambled to get herself and her impatient children bundled up and gather their bags. Anna would hardly be still and kept straining to see Santa.

Cooper and the Santa Claus took the children over to the sleigh, then Cooper returned to get his own things and to shut down and lock the truck. Santa helped Lacey with her bags.

Lacey paused in the shelter of the truck doorway. "Who are you?" she asked the pink-cheeked Santa.

"Just a retired old cabinetmaker who looks forward to a lot of fun every Christmas," he answered, a storybook twinkle in his eye. "For six years now I've been bringing gifts to the children here in our hollow. Some's free to the tykes who won't get anything else. Some's bought by parents, who also give a donation to our volunteer rescue squad as payment for me delivering. I was on my way home when I thought I'd better check out this stretch of highway. I've already hauled five people on up to the lodge."

"Busy night for Santa," Lacey said.

"Yep...most fun I've had in twenty years." The man chuckled. "Ain't found anyone hurt yet."

"Would you..." Lacey lifted the travel bag containing her presents. "Could *you* give the children and Cooper their gifts for me? I'll donate to your rescue squad."

"Surely." His cheeks were rosy in the dim light.

"How will we do it without them knowing?"

"Just set the bag down next to mine in the wagon, and leave the rest to old Santa."

"It's these...these three on the top," Lacey said eagerly.

Santa brought his sleigh to a jingling halt beneath the wide portico of the Mountain View Lodge. Then he distributed presents. Cooper felt a rush of pleasure when Anna squealed over the stuffed dog he'd bought her and Jon insisted on trying on his red jacket right then and there. But mostly it was the wonderment in Lacey's eyes as she held the crystal ball snow scene that moved him so. The eyes she turned to him had tears in them and were filled with so much pure happiness that he had to look away.

When Santa began handing out wrapped packages, Cooper realized that there were more presents than the ones he'd given the old man. With amused amazement, he realized Lacey had done the same as he. His amazement tripled when Santa placed a small package into his hands.

Lacey had bought him a present!

He stared at the bright red package with the gold ribbon. He hadn't had a real present for years; there'd been precious few of them throughout his entire life. He looked up to find Lacey gazing at him, a trembling smile on her lips, a warm light in her eyes. Feeling a whole lot the way he had when he'd lost control of the Kenworth, he smiled back and stuffed the package into his coat pocket. He'd wait until he was alone to open it.

"You'll get your puppy a bit later, Anna," Santa Claus promised just before he climbed into his sleigh. With jingles and creaks and a thunderous *"Merry Christmas!"* he drove away.

Cooper stood beside Lacey and watched the sleigh be swallowed up by the night. He felt a tug on his coat. It was Anna.

"I told you there was a Santa Claus," she said solemnly. "Do you believe now?"

"Yes, I believe," Cooper said.

"That's why you got a present," she said pertly, and broke into a run for the lodge's lobby. "I want to open my package!" she cried.

"Watch the steps, Anna!" Lacey called. Then she murmured playfully, "How do you suppose Santa knew where to find us?"

"Santa knows everything," Jon said with his usual know-it-all expression.

Chapter Six

Cooper rose before dawn, located a tow truck and had the Kenworth and Lacey and the kids rolling down the highway toward central North Carolina by nine o'clock. As the truck brought them ever closer to their destination, two things dominated Lacey's mind: greeting her father and saying goodbye to Cooper.

Did he care anything for her? she wondered as she sneaked glances at his profile. He wore the belt buckle she'd given him, had even said a quiet thank-you out of earshot of Anna. Maybe he was a bit mellower—certainly he seemed more familiar in the way he talked to her and the children—but other than that, there was nothing to indicate he held any intimate feelings toward her.

Why did she expect him to—because of the crystal snow scene he'd given her, the gifts for the children? Or because of her own feelings for him?

How in the world had she come to love him in only two short days? If he'd been as cordial during those two days as he was these past several hours, she could possibly understand it. But he hadn't—he'd been about as agreeable as a cactus, yet she'd been drawn to him from the very first moment.

The trip went perversely smoothly. For the first hour they were confined to one lane, but that one lane remained clear, and Cooper kept up almost normal speeds. Out of the mountains, the highway opened to two lanes. They stopped for breakfast and lunch, then spent the remaining hours serenaded by Christmas tunes on the radio and pacifying the two voices that kept asking, "Are we there yet?"

Lacey's nerves became tighter and tighter, so that when Cooper pulled the Kenworth off the highway exit for Pine Grove and asked which way, she fairly snapped at him.

"Just drop us over at that restaurant. I'll call my sister to come get us."

Cooper braked and gave her an exasperated look. "Which way, Lacey?"

"I'll call my sister."

"I'll take you."

He stared at her, and she stared back.

"Left," she said. "Five miles."

A lot had changed in Pine Grove in eleven years. A shopping mall had blossomed where she and her sister once had cut their Christmas trees. Huffner's country market was now a Super Save, and Fowler's TV Repair had become Fowler's Video Rental.

Soon, however, the Kenworth was rumbling its way slowly down the wide street of the graceful old neighborhood where Lacey had grown up. The big truck was definitely out of place, and Lacey worried over Cooper getting a ticket.

"Is this it?" Jon asked excitedly.

"Which one?" Anna said, craning her neck.

Lacey's gaze strained ahead. "There..." she said, pointing, and Cooper came to a rolling stop at the curb in front of her parents' large sloping yard. The sameness of it all was heartily reassuring.

Suddenly the children had lost their voices. They sat very still, staring up at the house. Lacey felt as if she couldn't move, even when she saw the front door opening, her parents stepping out onto the porch.

When Cooper said, "I'll go up and speak to them," she could do nothing but gape at him in astonishment.

Ignoring Lacey's expression, Cooper got out of the truck, paused and gave his hair a quick swipe with his hand. He felt pretty foolish and out of place, but he didn't want the kids going up there and being rejected by their grandpa right in front of their faces. For an instant the stark, clear memory of his own grandfather's forbidding face filled his mind. He pushed it aside.

Lacey's parents waited on the small front porch as Cooper loped up the carefully tended walk. Two-story, with a brick chimney and green shutters, the house breathed of substance and permanence.

Cooper came to a stop at the porch and took quick inventory of the people staring at him—a stern, no-nonsense type of man with silver hair and deep creases on either side of his turned-down mouth, the woman stylish and petite and standing one step behind her husband. A movement behind the curtains of a nearby window indicated onlookers inside. He returned his gaze to the silver-haired man.

"I've brought Lacey and your grandchildren for a visit," Cooper said. He watched the man's eyes grow small. "Will you welcome them?"

"Who are you?" the man asked after a long, silent moment.

"Just a friend," Cooper replied.

Another long pause, in which the man's expression changed to one of hope, and his eyes turned moist. "Please ask Lacey to come in," he said quietly.

Cooper hadn't known he'd been holding his breath until the man spoke those words.

The both dreaded and hoped-for moment had arrived, and Lacey didn't know how to cope. Her legs shook, and she accepted Cooper's steadying hand in getting down from the truck. Then joy burst within her when her mother came hurrying down the walk with open arms, making it so much easier.

Finally she was facing her father, seeing the changes, recognizing that some things would never change. He had aged but was as stern as always.

"Daddy, these are my children," Lacey said, standing in front of him, her shoulders squared, Jon and Anna on either side of her.

She couldn't remember ever seeing her father cry, but now a tear slipped down his cheek. Lacey blinked, her vision growing almost too blurry to see. When her father opened his arms, she rushed to embrace him, feeling his rough face against hers, his coarse silver hair. "Oh, Daddy, I've missed you," she said in a hoarse whisper, and then she cried into his white dress shirt.

"Welcome home," her father murmured gruffly. He held her tight, then, self-consciously averting his gaze, he pulled away and turned to the children, pure pleasure lighting his moist eyes. "So, these are my grandchildren...."

Then bedlam broke out, with Beth and her husband and children pouring from the house, everyone hugging and talking excitedly. Lacey pulled away from Beth and anxiously sought Cooper, fearful he would slip away in all the commotion before she could speak to him. She had to thank him—and more. She was bursting with passion. For the moment she felt bold and courageous, enough so to tackle the whole world. She could tell Cooper how she felt about him, self-consciousness and fear be damned. She would tell him, and surely he would feel the same. He just had to.

Her anxiousness vanished when she saw her mother had corralled Cooper; Emily Sawyer was never one to forget the propriety of asking a guest to stay at least for coffee.

Lacey stepped over and boldly grabbed Cooper's hand, tugging him forward. She smiled broadly at Beth's raised eyebrows. "Cooper, I'd like you to meet my parents, my family."

Cooper sat talking with Lacey's father, Leon Sawyer, drinking a third cup of coffee and finishing off a second piece of pecan pie—and knowing he had to get gone. The way Lacey kept looking at him—had been looking at him throughout the day—had him all churned up inside, like a wildcat caught in a net.

He felt almost overwhelmed by the rest of the crowd, too. He'd rarely been surrounded by a family like this, showing so much care for one another—and for him, simply because he was a friend of Lacey's. Of course, everyone kept giving him those secretive looks, as if they shared some private joke with him. Everyone except Leon, who looked at him as if he was trying to guess his coat size. Once Leon asked him how long he'd known Lacey. Cooper could tell his answer didn't set too well with the man, and it was as if Leon had to bite his tongue not to speak about it. Cooper saw the love between Lacey and her father, but he saw the personality clash as well.

"You'll stay for dinner?" Emily Sawyer asked him in her pleasantly modulated voice. "We have plenty of leftovers from the big meal at noon today."

That was his out, and Cooper took it. "No... thank you, ma'am." He rose, looking around for his coat. "I have to get this haul up to Washington."

When Jon and Anna heard Cooper was leaving, they raced to get their coats so they could walk him to his truck. Lacey would rather have gone alone with him, but the children had grown fond of Cooper; it wouldn't be fair to deny them their goodbyes. Jon shook Cooper's hand, Anna gave a little wave, then Lacey ordered them back up to the house. "I'll be right along," she assured them.

The clouds had faded, and the sky was a clear, crisp blue fading into evening. Lacey stood in front of Cooper, feeling the buoyant courage that had sprung up so readily in the emotional moments of the special afternoon evaporating like air out of a hot balloon.

She looked at him, then down at the mushy snow. How should she tell him her feelings? What words could she use? Would he think her a fool? Did he care at all? Would she be more embarrassed than she had ever been in her life?"

Cooper opened the truck door and paused.

"Thanks so much for the ride out," Lacey said. She stared up, searching his dark eyes for any sign that she should speak her heart. She found none.

Cooper nodded. "You want me to stop and get you in a week for the ride back?"

Her tongue seemed to swell. "I . . ." It *is* Christmas, she thought. A magical time. And you might as well tell him because you'll live with regret if you don't. "Do you want us to ride back with you?"

He gave a shrug and looked over her head before looking back down at her. "It's no problem for me. I'll just take a few local loads up around D.C. and start back in a week. I'll be heading to Albuquerque anyway."

"I asked if you wanted us to come."

He stared at her a long time, and the sorrow that came into his eyes stabbed her.

"You're asking me for something I can't give, Lacey. I don't have it in me to give." His words fell as pebbles dropped into a pond, and with each one, Lacey's heart seemed to crack.

She stared into his eyes and frantically sought her mind for words to make him understand, make him see the beauty that could be between them.

"Maybe it's more what I can give you, Cooper." Her heart beat so fast she thought it would jump right out of her chest. "I love you." She watched him, held her breath and thought wordless prayers.

Cooper looked at her. His eyes softened, and Lacey's hope soared. Then his eyes turned bleak.

"Lacey, I'm just a burned-out old driver. You and me...we're like water and diesel fuel, we ain't gonna mix. You don't see things like they are, only like you want them to be. And life just ain't like that."

"It can be, if you let it." Why wouldn't he see? Why did he have to be so pigheaded and cynical?

"No..." He shook his head.

Lacey knew he didn't believe. Hadn't he told her that before? He didn't believe in things like Santa Claus, or Christmas, or love. He didn't believe there could be a "them." Probably didn't even *want* there to be a "them." And here she was, pressing him.

Stop it! she told herself firmly. Shoving her fists into her coat pockets, she stepped back, squared her shoulders and forced a smile. She would not cry; she'd die first.

"Thanks so much for bringing us...and for going up to check out Daddy for me." Her smile felt frozen. "That was very kind of you. We'll be fine...and we'll ride back on the bus."

Something flashed across his face, pain maybe, but Lacey couldn't see very well. It surprised her when he reached out and gripped her arm.

"See you back at Gerald's?" he said.

"Sure . . . see you then."

Late that night, when everyone was asleep, Lacey slipped down to the kitchen for some warm milk. While pouring it into a cup, she heard her father's footsteps.

"Can't you sleep?" he asked, entering the kitchen.

She smiled. "Too many thoughts about today, I guess." Her father looked at her a minute, then reached for the pan and milk. "I'll make it, Daddy. Sit down. You're not supposed to stand on that leg." At his look she said, "Beth told me about the problem with your veins last week."

"You'd better not have come back just to plague me like the others—to pander to me," he said sharply, but he sat.

"I didn't, Daddy. I came home to make up and to have my father again. And it was big of me, too." She was rewarded by his slow smile.

He hugged her, and she loved it. "Are some of those thoughts whirling around in your head about that young man who brought you here today?" he asked.

Lacey nodded and looked down into her milk. "Some."

"When you were younger," he said, "you never talked to me about the boys you liked. Guess it's a bit late to start."

"Yes, Daddy." She touched his arm. "But I love you."

He looked embarrassed and reached for the photo album she'd given him. He opened it, and as they drank their milk, he asked questions about each picture, as if hungry to catch up on his grandchildren's lives.

"You doing all right out there in New Mexico?" her father asked, turning his attention from the photos.

"Do you make enough to support you and the kids as well?"

She looked at him, realizing he'd know immediately if she lied. "Sometimes the money is tight, but we eat well and have a nice apartment in a friendly neighborhood. I like waitressing, Daddy. I'm good at taking care of people that way. The kids have everything they need and plenty of extras. We're doing okay."

"You have to think of the future, Lace...." When he saw her expression, he stopped and raised an eyebrow. "If you'd like to come here to live, you'd be welcome. I'd ... I'd like it, Lacey."

Lacey moved to lean against his shoulder. "Thanks so much, Dad. So very much. I'll think about it."

It had been a wonderful Christmas, she thought when she finally climbed into bed. One she would remember for a long time. Sitting cross-legged, she ran the brush Jon had given her in long strokes through her hair. It was a lovely brush-and-comb set, yet what Lacey held most dear was the look of love on Jon's face when he'd presented it, a gift bought with his own hard-earned money.

The crystal ball snow scene Cooper had given her sat on the nightstand. Lacey gazed at the small globe, then lifted and shook it to watch the "snow" fall gently onto the tree. Then she pressed the glass ball to her heart and squeezed her eyes shut against tears.

She'd never forget her time with Cooper and counted it a joy, if a bittersweet one. She wouldn't have missed caring for him for the world. She wondered when the hurt would go away. And how she would face him back at Gerald's.

* * *

The days that followed were good. It snowed again, and Anna and Jon spent several afternoons sledding with their cousins at a nearby hill. Lacey's mother threw a party, inviting old friends and family. There were long girl-talks with Beth, companionable walks with her mother and stubborn arguments with her father, although he did most of the arguing. Lacey simply listened. She'd learned a few things in eleven years.

Her father fumed when Lacey decided her family's home was in Albuquerque now. He didn't understand why she wouldn't come home to live, where it would be a lot easier for her. When she explained that she and the children had their own home out west, that she had a good job, good friends, the children's school, he pointed out her lack of money and security, and most of all, family.

"You and Mama are only a phone call away," she told him, to which he grumbled irritably.

He would help with money, he told her, and if she had any sense at all, she would take it. She told him he could begin by lending her the bus fare back, which led to still more raving about how she didn't have a decent savings account. Her mother mentioned that her father hadn't had any savings account at Lacey's age.

Though she knew she was being foolish, Lacey couldn't help gazing out the window, looking for a maroon Kenworth to come rolling up the street. Beth found her at the window on New Year's Eve, a traditionally quiet time at their house.

"You hoping he'll come back?" Beth asked.

At her voice, Lacey turned, somewhat sheepishly. "I guess I am ... silly of me." She rubbed her arms. "Thanks for this sweater, sis. I love it."

"You're welcome." Beth flopped onto the couch. "It's not necessarily silly. Maybe he will come back."

Lacey shook her head, bent and prodded the fire with the poker. "It would be more probable for it to snow in July," she said.

"It has snowed in July," Beth stated. "In Vermont, I believe, back in the eighteen-hundreds. So you see, miracles do happen. Is he a good man?"

Lacey smiled softly. "Yes, I think so. He's just so...so ornery."

"But you love him?"

Lacey shrugged but remained silent. Somehow it seemed her heart couldn't bear to admit it, for it would make the pain worse.

"Go ahead and hope," Beth said then.

"What good will that do?" Lacey asked, hugging herself.

"It will get you through tonight—and maybe he will come back."

Lacey tried to smile for her sister, who was lovingly and loyally trying to make her feel better. But maybe the only way to deal with her pain was to accept that Cooper could never feel what she did and put it behind her. It was only a fleeting incident in her life. One that touched her deeply, one that changed her, but not one meant to last.

Was it too late? Cooper asked himself for the twentieth time. If it was, he was stuck with this stupid puppy that had chewed up one of his best leather gloves and half of the small basket in which it now slept in the sleeper compartment.

He hadn't even left the Sawyers' neighborhood on Christmas Day when he'd begun wondering about him and Lacey. All the way up to D.C. and during the week, when he found some short hauls to keep him in the area, he'd told himself he had plenty of time to think about it—*it* being his feelings for Lacey.

But for the last two hours, he'd begun to wonder if Lacey might have changed her mind during the past week. She might have met an old boyfriend. She might even have already left for Albuquerque.

He'd feel real stupid if she'd changed her mind. If he'd called her, he could have been embarrassed over the telephone, which was preferable to being embarrassed face-to-face with her. But he didn't think something like this could be discussed over the phone. He had to see her, talk to her and risk feeling a fool. The thought made his palms sweat, his mouth taste bad.

He thought of her green eyes, her contagious smile and the way she'd had the guts to tell him she loved him. She'd spoken the words plainly, not murmured them during the hot seconds of passion, when a person might say anything, truth or not.

She loved him. Lacey wouldn't have said it if it hadn't been true. But then, he'd been fooled before.

Cooper wasn't certain what he was feeling. He knew only that he wanted to be with Lacey, to see her smile all for him. Good grief, he even wanted to see the kids. He wasn't certain as to the why of any of it. Or the wisdom.

All the questions whirled in his mind as he pulled the Kenworth to a stop at the curb in front of the Sawyers' graceful house. The truck's engine purred smoothly; Cooper stared up at the house. Lights shone from every room, and he wondered if they were having a New Year's Eve party. He cursed himself for not thinking of that. But no cars filled the driveway, and everything seemed quiet.

It would help a lot if Lacey would happen to see him and come out to meet him, he thought as he opened the truck door.

A sound drew Lacey from the table where she played chess with her father. The children upstairs, she thought, though she went to look out the window anyway.

When she saw the glimmer of maroon beneath the street lamp, the breath rushed from her lungs. *Cooper!* Thinking maybe it was her imagination, she closed her eyes, then opened them again. Cooper had said she looked at the world through rose-colored glasses, and yes, she did. But even she hadn't truly believed he would return.

Turning, Lacey strode to the door, then ran out into the night, her father's call "Lacey?" following her.

She ran halfway down the walk and then stopped. Maybe Cooper hadn't come back for her. Maybe she'd left something in his truck, or he'd just decided to give her a friendly lift, or...

He'd circled the front of the truck and now stood at the curb. Lacey waited, her heart pounding. Slowly he walked forward across the snow-covered lawn. Then he was walking faster, as if in eager anticipation! Lacey ran toward him, and when he opened his arms, she went to him and buried her face in his jacket.

"Come out of the snow," he said at last, leading her down toward the shoveled sidewalk.

He stopped beneath the streetlight. His arm remained securely around her, and Lacey looked up, wondering at what was happening. She touched his cheek and waited.

"I don't know what's happened to me," he said. The confusion on his face tore at her heart, yet pleasurably so. He moved in front of her and cupped her face in his hands. "I just know I couldn't leave without you and the kids. Yes, even the kids." He gave a hoarse chuckle, then his brow furrowed. "Will you go back with me, Lacey? Can we . . . can we see about us?"

"Oh, Cooper . . ." Her words caught in her throat, and she was crying and laughing at once. "What's happened to you is love, darling." She wound her arms around his neck. "And I love you," she whispered just before his lips crushed hers.

When at last he lifted his lips, Lacey had to gasp for breath. She snuggled against him, unwilling to break the contact. Her mind whirled with the wonder of it all. Then she opened her eyes and found herself staring at the front of the Kenworth. The Christmas lights were still there, but they no longer said, Bah, Humbug.

H-O-squiggle-*O*-squiggle-*O*. Why, it said Ho, Ho, Ho, if one was imaginative.

"I had trouble with the letters," Cooper said, stroking her hair.

Lacey, tears of joy streaming down her face, began to pound his chest. "You believe! You believe! You believe in love now!"

Cooper shook his head, as if he couldn't comprehend it himself. "Yes," he said with a slow smile. "I do."

Slipping a hand onto the back of her neck, he held her firmly and brought his lips to hers in a warm, seductive kiss that promised much more to come.

Then he lifted his head and murmured, "Santa sent Anna's puppy by way of me."

*   *   *   *   *